Walter Herries Pollock

The Picture's Secret

A story - to which is added an episode in the life of Mr. Latimer

Walter Herries Pollock

The Picture's Secret
A story - to which is added an episode in the life of Mr. Latimer

ISBN/EAN: 9783337332495

Printed in Europe, USA, Canada, Australia, Japan

Cover: Foto ©Andreas Hilbeck / pixelio.de

More available books at **www.hansebooks.com**

THE PICTURE'S SECRET.

A Story.

*To which is added an Episode in the Life of
Mr. Latimer.*

BY

WALTER HERRIES POLLOCK.

London :

REMINGTON AND CO.,

New Bond Street, W.

———

1883.

CHARLES H. E. BROOKFIELD.

THE PICTURE'S SECRET.

CHAPTER I.

CECIL, thirteenth Earl Falcon, was a man of somewhat peculiar character. Those who knew him little set him down as reserved and cold : those who knew him well said that he had deep passions seldom revealed. If the storms of passion did in truth ever attack him, their force was spent in unseen caverns of his mind : no visible wave rolled on the surface of his nature, no convulsion troubled its calmness ; but that was no proof that convulsions did not exist in the depths below. Some of his friends attributed this seldom varied evenness of demeanour to the strength of his will ; others said that his devotion to music exhausted all his power of feeling. Certainly he had an extraordinary talent and a surprising love for this art, and was never so happy as when he could be left for hours together to follow out the play of his fancy and give momentary life to his reveries in the notes struck by his master hand. For society he cared little, although he must always have been distinguished in it, as well for his personal qualities as for his inherited name and wealth. People who met him for the first time seldom took any strong liking to him, but his manner had a dignity and grace which commanded their attention. He on his side was vexed whenever he was obliged to go into society; and he was no better pleased than usual when one night he felt it necessary to appear at a ball given by his old friend Mrs. Norman. Here, just as he was beginning to congratulate himself on

the prospect of soon slipping away, his attention was caught by a girl dancing on the
opposite side of the room. The musicians
were playing a languid, dreamy German
waltz, and the singular grace with which her
movements seemed to respond to the spirit
of the music first attracted his eye. Then
as she and her partner swung round the
room towards him, he observed her more
closely, and noticed a kind of childish appealing look in her face, a look as of one who
sought some strong support to lean on, being
too weak to face the turmoil of the world
alone. There was also a fascination not only
in the look, but also in the small pliant figure,
which was undefined, and therefore to a man
of Lord Falcon's fastidious temperament the
more attractive, perhaps, because it presented
no salient point for the critical faculty to lay
hold of and find fault with. In the claims

made by established beauties to admiration Lord Falcon generally found some defect; either the face was somewhere out of drawing, or, if faultless in that respect, was spoilt by a want of meaning. The attraction of this girl, if indefinable, was far from being insignificant: as she passed the spot where Falcon stood her eyes sent forth a glance in his direction, and their look filled him with a feeling of perplexed admiration: they seemed to remind him of something beautiful, of what he could not tell; they had also a hidden fire, he thought, an untamed expression which was at variance with his first impression. He looked, wondered, and looked again; and at the end of the next dance he went up to his cousin, Arthur Vane.

"Who is that girl with whom you were dancing just before this, Arthur?" he asked.

"What?" said the other; "is Saul among

the prophets? Are you asking a woman's name? Can it be that your devotion has wandered from Beethoven and Mozart to the things of this earth?"

Falcon smiled with a certain gravity of demeanour which belonged even to his smiles. " Cannot one ask a name without being suspected of a particular interest in its owner?" he said.

" *One* can, no doubt; but scarcely you, Falcon, who have never done such a thing before. But I am glad you are curious about her, for I think you would like her."

" Do you? Why?"

" I can scarcely tell you why. But you have a way of taking to anything that is peculiar, and I think she is that. There is something curious and unlike ordinary life in her look and manner. I do not know what to call it—barbaric, perhaps."

"Barbaric!" repeated Falcon, musingly. "No! I do not think it is quite that."

"You seem to have observed her closely," said Vane with a laugh; "but shall I introduce you to her? That will make it easier for you to discover what she is."

"I shall be very happy," said Falcon; "but you have not yet told me her name."

"There is one good reason for that, which is, that I don't know it myself. You know how difficult it is to catch names; but I can easily find it out. Come, we will go and look for her."

They began to make their way through the rooms with this object, but during their passage Falcon came face to face with Miss Norman, the daughter of the house. Greeting developed into conversation, which presently turned to Falcon's pet subject, music; and finding an empty seat next to Miss Norman, he occupied it, leaving Vane to continue his search alone.

Miss Norman was a fine musician, and Falcon was always glad to meet her, if only for that reason ; but, apart from that, he had a liking for her, which her mother sometimes hoped might develop into a stronger feeling. Of this, however, there was no chance; Vane was quite right when he implied that his cousin had never cared much for any woman. The fact was that he had little sympathy with the everyday life of the world ; he preferred his own existence of dreamy imaginations which it was his chief delight to interpret in music. But in Miss Norman's society he generally found some pleasure : she was unaffected and clever, did not vex him with trivialities, and could criticise his compositions with interest and taste. Thus it happened that, relinquishing for a time the purpose with which he had begun to walk through the rooms, he remained talking to Miss Norman, and ended by dancing with her, more for the purpose of carrying on their conversation than anything else.

Vane, meanwhile, had found the object of his search, and was dancing with her again. His curiosity was aroused concerning her, partly on his own account, partly because of the interest which Falcon seemed to take in her; and he looked at her carefully more than once to discover wherein lay her attraction. Her features had no striking beauty or peculiarity: they were rather small and irregular; her dress and demeanour, when analysed, could not be said to differ specially from those of others; yet there was something unusual and striking about her. Perhaps it might be in her eyes that the charm, if charm it was, should be found; they had a strange look, he thought, as of one who saw more than was visible to other mortal eyes. Even as he thought so she looked up and met his glance with a gaze so keen and piercing that his own dropped before it, and he felt confused, as if detected in a guilty action. He recovered himself quickly, and said to her—

"When I came to look for you just now I was impelled by purely unselfish motives, and you see virtue has brought its reward for once."

"Has it?" she said, "and what was your unselfish motive?"

"My cousin Falcon was anxious to be introduced to you."

"Lord Falcon! I have heard of him. Is not he very musical? Is he here now?"

"Yes," said Vane, "there he is, just opposite to us."

She looked across the room to where

Falcon was standing, deep in conversation with Miss Norman. He was bending down towards her, and his face, usually marked by a grave stillness, was lighted up with an eager interest. Any one looking at them might have thought that they were deep in a flirtation, or in something yet more serious; whereas, in fact, they were discussing a great master's rendering of a certain violin solo. Falcon's grand manner gave a picturesque aspect to a group ordinary in itself; and it may have been the sense of this which caused Vane's partner to look steadily at the pair. Vane, observing this, said, in a somewhat mischievous tone—

"They seem to get on very well together."

She, without varying the direction of her eyes, replied quickly—

"Yes, is not she Miss Norman? I know her very slightly."

"She is," replied Vane; "they are old friends, and may be more some day, people say. But I believe people are wrong, as they usually are."

"Do you?" she asked, with a rapid look of inquiry, and before he could answer, said with a little soft laugh, "Shall we go on again?"

The next pause in the dance brought them close to Miss Norman and Falcon; and he, looking up for a moment from his conversation encountered once again the eyes which had so strangely impressed him. Again he wondered at the curious mixture of expressions which he thought he detected in them, but failed to define. As he wondered and his thoughts strayed into a vague reverie, Vane and his partner swept past him, and he was recalled to himself by hearing close to him a slight laugh, low in tone, but of a penetrating quality, and seeing the graceful turn of a head disappearing in the crowd. This was the last dance of the evening, and Falcon, having seen his partner safely into her mother's custody, went in search of the girl who had been dancing with his cousin, but found that she had disappeared. In the hall he fell in with his brother-in-law, Sir Harry Grey, and they walked away together.

"Can you tell me," said Falcon, presently, "who was the girl with whom Arthur was dancing?"

"A little girl in white, with rather an odd look?" asked the other.

Falcon nodded.

"Oh, yes! I thought Arthur seemed rather hit by her."

Falcon paused a moment, and then replied with an asperity unusual to him—

"Arthur is never hit by anybody; he flirts

a little with every one, and never goes much deeper. He danced with her twice, it is true; but he has probably forgotten all about her by this time. He does not even know her name, I believe. What is her name, and who is she? There is something rather interesting about her, I think."

"Yes," said Sir Harry, who in the quiet content of his cigar, had not noticed Falcon's unusual excitement. "She is an odd girl, I fancy. Miss von Waldheim her name is."

"A German name," said Falcon.

"Yes, but the family have been in England for some time, and are practically English now. Her father is a painter; you must have seen his pictures."

"I have," said Falcon, "he paints very imaginative pictures, if I remember right."

"Imaginative, just so," said Sir Harry; "that's what people call it; they seem to me

poor stuff, but I daresay I'm wrong. I
must say when I go to look at pictures I like
to see something that I've really seen or
might see some day; and who ever expects
to see such things as von Waldheim paints?
Goblins and ghosts, and a lot of stuff of that
sort; very well painted I've no doubt, but it
doesn't interest me. He's a good fellow,
though, von Waldheim, as far as I've seen
him."

"And his daughter?" asked Falcon.

"I can't make her out. Sometimes when I
talk to her I think she's a perfect baby; and
sometimes I think she's laughing at me all the
time. But she's a nice girl, too; she has pretty
ways with her; kitten-like kind of ways."

"Ah," said Falcon, "that is how it strikes
you, is it?"

"Yes, that is how it strikes me," continued
Harry; "they say she leads her father rather

a life at times, but he is devoted to his Lilith. Odd name Lilith, isn't it ? "

" Very odd," said Falcon ; " it is in the legend the name of Adam's first wife. The word really means, I think, ' before the morning dawn.' "

" Just so," said Sir Harry. " They say her father was painting one of his queer pictures when she was born, and would call her Lilith after somebody or something in the picture. The mother didn't like it; said it was a name fit only for a heathen, and was sure to bring the child ill-luck and ruin ; but Lilith she was called all the same."

" And Lilith she is called still. A strange name, certainly—and a strange girl probably," said Falcon.

" Yes, a strange girl. I daresay you would get on with her. If you like I can take you any day to von Waldheim's studio."

"Thank you," said Falcon, "I daresay I will come. Here I turn off. Good night."

Falcon went home, opened his piano, and sitting down, let his fingers wander over the keys at the bidding of the vague thoughts which hovered in his brain. He played Beethoven's 'Moonlight Sonata,' and the soft ripple of the melody reminded him of Lilith von Waldheim's graceful movement in the dance; he struck into a wild mazurka of Chopin, and recalled the strange look which she had darted at him; he changed to Mendelssohn's 'Midsummer Night's Dream,' and still her image rose before him. As the airy delicate notes sounded he seemed to see troops of fairies,—Peasblossom, Mustard-seed, Cobweb, and their attendant rout—flitting hither and thither in the chequered moonlight, and in their midst stood Titania in the likeness of Lilith. Perhaps it was, in truth, the thought of her latent in his mind which led him to play everything wild and fantastic which he could remember rather than that the eerie melodies recalled her to him ; but in the mood which then possessed him he was little inclined to make nice distinctions between cause and effect, and the most marked impression on his mind when he left the piano and went to bed was that this girl had produced a singular effect upon his imagination.

Lilith meanwhile had gone home with her father to his house in Kensington. Mr. von Waldheim was a man of a dignified presence, tall and upright, with keen dark eyes, which looked out from under heavy brows, whose blackness contrasted with his white hair and beard. It was this contrast as much as anything else which gave a wildness to his appearance, and favoured the report that he was afflicted with a most violent temper, which his daughter's presence alone had power to subdue. For her he was all kindness: he humoured her every fancy; when they were seen together it was very easy to understand how the father, from whose hand one might naturally expect pictures of a dashing or ferocious character, came to paint those bright, poetical works of fancy by which he was chiefly known. It was possible in the hints of subtle mockery, which he sometimes introduced into his pictures, to discover a trace of the bitter temper with which he was credited, but the general effect of his paintings was light and ethereal. When the father and daughter arrived at home that night—

"Well, fairy," said Mr. von Waldheim, "did you have a nice ball? With whom did you dance? Any new partners?"

"Yes," said Lilith, "there was a Mr. Vane, who was rather nice, I thought. And there ought to have been another: his cousin, Lord Falcon; but he was stopped on the way when he was coming to be introduced to me. Do you know Lord Falcon, dear papa?"

"No; I know about him; a man of considerable power, I hear, especially in the line of music: he has composed several songs of a rather sombre nature, which I believe corresponds with his own. At least he is said to be very reserved."

"I wonder why people are ever reserved," said Lilith, reflectively; "it seems to me that it would be much better if everyone were to tell out what was in them."

"If everyone were like you, fairy, that plan might possibly answer. But while there is so much that had better not be told in people's minds, it might lead to confusion and evil consequences."

"Is there much that ought not to be told?" asked Lilith, with an air of simplicity. "I suppose there is, but it seems a great pity. Why should it be so?"

"Don't trouble your little head about such things, my pet. Good night."

CHAPTER II.

Next day Vane came to see Falcon, and found him studying and correcting a MS. score of a composition.

"Still devoted to the old idol ?" he cried. "I thought you seemed likely to go after strange goddesses last night."

"What do you mean ?" asked Falcon, looking up for a moment, and then returning to his score.

"I fancy you might have found a counter attraction in Miss von Waldheim."

"Oh ! you have found out her name ?" said Falcon.

"So have you, it seems," replied Vane, laughing, "or else some occult sympathy led you to guess whom I meant. Such things exist, I believe ; you do not think so, of course; you are too strong-minded, and attribute all such ideas to a weak intellect or a feeble constitution. Whether she is a goddess or not, as I dare say she may be, I think there is something strange about her. What do you think?"

"I?" said Falcon; "why should I trouble myself to think on such a subject?"

"I do not know why you should do so," replied Vane, "but I am tolerably certain that you have thought about her. You displayed an interest in her last night which I have seldom observed in you before; I saw you looking at her with, to say the least of it, attention, more than once."

Falcon rose and put away his music sheet. Every form of deceit, however slight, was distasteful to him, and he now spoke out exactly that which was in him.

"Well," he said, "I did watch her with

attention ; she did interest me ; this I confess ; is my confession very terrible ? "

" Coming from you it is perhaps a little
alarming," said Vane, laughingly, and then
catching, with quick sympathy, a touch of
dislike to this jesting tone in Falcon's face,
he went on—" If you really are at all interested about her I am glad ; it seems to me
that you care too little for anything in the
outer world, and the von Waldheims are
thoroughly artistic people, and would please
you, I think. The father asked me last night
to come and look at his pictures any day I
liked, and I do not suppose there would be
much difficulty about your coming with
me."

" Thank you," said Falcon, with some deliberation. " Grey, with whom I walked back
last night, has already offered to take me to
Mr. von Waldheim's studio."

" Oh ! " replied Vane, in a tone which implied that if he had said more it would have been, " Has it gone so far as that ? "

He walked about the room a little in a restless way, and then said—

" Have you anything to do this afternoon, Falcon ? "

" That means," said Falcon, with his grave smile, " will you come to the von Waldheims with me ? I have no objection to gratifying you so far."

" Ah ! you are always laughing at me for what you call my impressionable temperament ; but for once you are mistaken. In the case of Miss von Waldheim, I am influenced by the merest curiosity—as no doubt you are yourself."

To this shaft Falcon made no reply, and appeared to be busy in arranging his music for a few moments, at the end of which he said—

" We may as well go now as at any other time."

" Yes," said Vane, " it is a good light for looking at pictures, is it not ? Let us go and call for Grey."

Upon this the two set out.

Vane certainly deserved the character for being impressionable, of which in his ex-cuses to Falcon he had accused himself ; but it was equally true that Lilith von Wald-heim had not produced upon his susceptible nature that effect which women of various kinds of fascination were apt to produce. He felt no inclination to flirt with her ; no nascent tenderness ; he experienced only, as he had said, a curiosity about her. He wondered himself at this, knowing to some extent his own weakness for falling a little in love with every new face which possessed any attraction ; and he wondered the more because he saw a man so difficult to please as Falcon betraying a certain amount of excitement about a girl in whom his fastidious judgment might easily find defects.

Thus his curiosity was awakened, as well to discover why Falcon took so great an interest in her, as to inquire on his own account into her character and belongings. Falcon, on his part, could not define the feelings which led him to agree so quickly to Vane's plan of going to Mr. von Waldheim's studio; he was conscious that his usual equanimity was a little ruffled, but could not probably, had he been so inclined, have traced and analysed the disturbing influences which were at work.

The reflections of both men, however, were sufficiently absorbing to keep them nearly silent until they arrived at Sir Harry Grey's house, where they were received by Lady Emmeline Grey, commonly known as Lady

Emmy, Falcon's sister. For her her brother entertained a deep affection ; for her and in her service he would undertake anything, even when it involved leaving his piano and his music in the very heat of successful composition ; and an expression of singular softness and sweetness came into his face as he greeted her, and said—

"How do you do, dear Emmy? We missed you much at the ball last night."

As she began to answer, Sir Harry came into the room.

"How are you, Falcon? How do, Arthur?" he said. "I suppose you two mean to go to von Waldheim's studio. Well, I'm always glad to go there, not that I care about his pictures, but he's a deuced pleasant fellow, von Waldheim, and that little girl of his amuses me. You'll be fighting over her I expect, you two."

He chuckled contentedly as he concluded his speech ; but Falcon looked grave as usual ; Vane made a quick gesture of dissent, and Lady Emmy said—

" You should not put such ideas into young men's heads, Harry. Falcon, of course, is going to look at Mr. von Waldheim's studies, and as for Arthur, I doubt if he can care for anyone up to the point of quarrelling."

" Well," said Sir Harry, " I was right in my guess as to your intentions, at any rate ; so let us be going."

They started accordingly for Kensington. Before they went, Lady Emmy looked hard at her brother, and said—

" Take care of yourself, Cecil," to which he only replied—

" Dear little Emmy ! always thinking for others."

It was a bright spring day, such as comes

once in a while to enliven the spirits of those who are condemned to dwell in a region for the most part dark and smoke-weighted. Birds were singing cheerily among the early leaves as they walked through Kensington Gardens; and the sun shone with a brilliance which is so rare in London, that it seems misplaced and garish when it first appears. Thus, while their walk was pleasant and in-spiriting, the change from the prevailing brightness without to the carefully arranged light and shade within the studio which they entered came just at the right time to pro-duce an agreeable effect.

It has often been said that rooms bear the impress of their owner's individuality, if he has any; and the aspect of Mr. von Wald-heim's studio argued that whoever had planned it possessed an original taste. The floor was polished and uncarpeted, save for a large soft rug in front of the fireplace, whereon a Persian cat was stretched lazily at full length, blinking its large eyes in sleepy contentment. In one corner was a tall Japanese screen covered with quaint devices, which Vane, on close inspection, discovered with a little disgust to be elaborate representations of the Japanese idea of hell ; in another, behind a velvet-covered table, littered with all kinds of *bric-à-brac*, Dresden china, miniatures by Cosway, and Louis Quatorze snuff-boxes, stood a large figure, the white drapery of which somehow suggested the idea of a shroud to Vane's imagination. On an easel was an unfinished picture, which represented " Queen Mab and her Court." The central figure was evidently drawn from Lilith ; she sat in an attitude of fantastic grace on an airy throne, receiving the homage of her courtiers. Falcon looked long at the picture.

"That is wonderfully like your daughter, Mr. von Waldheim," he said, presently, "and allow me to say an exquisite picture."

The artist gave a quick look at him from under his heavy brows, and said—

"Here is another picture which I think will interest you."

He led the way to the fireplace, over which hung a large picture, of which Falcon did not at once comprehend the meaning. It represented a mouutain landscape seen by moonlight; all of which, save the foreground, was obscured by driving mist and clouds; in the foreground were two men leaning against a projecting rock, and looking intently into the mass of wreathing vapour. Fixing his gaze upon these two figures, about neither of whom there was at first sight anything striking or peculiar, Falcon observed that the face of the one bore an expression of deep unrest and hardly

mastered sorrow, while the careless amusement visible in the bearing and countenance
of the other had something painful and mocking in the force of its contrast.

Following with his eye the direction of
their glance, the spectator perceived that the
eddying clouds which crept and rolled across
the mountain, in the dim light of the background, were full of grotesque shapes, so near
akin in colour and consistency to the drift
itself as to seem part of the sphere which they
inhabited.   Here might be seen a long-nosed
fiend, bowing low, with gestures of extrava-
gant admiration, to an old witch ; there, a
couple of graceful sprites dancing swiftly
together through the light vapour ; farther
on again was a group of strange phantoms,
which might be either living beings moving
in the world of elves, or mere images, formed
out of the whirling mist, according to the

spectator's fancy ; over all the skill of the painter had cast a wonderful air of life and motion. In the very centre of the picture was a rift in the clouds, through which a ray of moonlight streamed on to a woman's figure draped in long gauzy robes, from whom the surrounding goblins and witches seemed to have shrunk in terror or subjection, so that she walked entirely alone. Her face could not be distinguished ; but the artist had infused a spirit of disdain into her attitude, which would by itself account for her solitude. While Falcon continued to look closely at the painting, the artist said—

" That is the picture on which I was at work when my daughter was born, and I called her after it in a manner ; you have recognised the subject already, no doubt."

Before Falcon could reply, Sir Harry and Vane, who had been looking together at the

D

studies and sketches which hung round the wall, came up.

"Strange picture that, isn't it, Falcon ?" said Sir Harry. "Scene on the Brocken with Faust and Mephistopheles looking on. You've read *Faust,* of course, and will know all about it ; I haven't. I don't go in for that sort of thing."

"You have seen the opera of *Faust?*" said Mr. von Waldheim.

"Yes, yes ; I've seen the opera scores of times ; but there's nothing like that in it. I like the opera. I like to see that fellow, Faure, when they hold up the crosses of their swords at him."

"Yes," said Vane, "that is fine. I see, Mr. von Waldheim, you have chosen the moment of Lilith's appearance for your picture. Retzsch, if I am not mistaken, has taken the apparition of Gretchen for his outline drawing."

"Yes," replied the artist, "it may have been because I was afraid of copying Retzsch; but I think the real fact was, that the idea started into my head. A picture strikes me suddenly, and takes possession of me until I have transferred it to canvas. Whether it is worth the trouble of transferring or not, is a question which never occurs to me at the time."

"This one was well worth it," said Falcon, who was still looking at it. At this moment the door opened and Lilith von Waldheim entered the room with the peculiar light floating step which had struck Falcon as being so graceful at the ball. A smile of triumph lit up her face for a moment when she perceived his presence; but she scarcely raised her eyes to his when her father introduced him, and she turned almost immediately to Vane, saying—

"I hope you have been admiring papa's

pictures. But of course you have, because
you have good taste—at least I have heard
so."

"I am glad you have heard so much good
of me, Miss von Waldheim. I can bear out
your kind expression in this, that I have been
admiring Mr. von Waldheim's pictures very
much."

"That is quite right," said Lilith. "I
shall not ask Sir Harry for his opinion, because he always pretends to know nothing
about them. I believe it is only to save himself the trouble of talking."

"Fact is," said Sir Harry to Vane, in an
undertone, "I like some pictures well enough,.
but I never can see anything to care about
in von Waldheim's; so I'm always obliged
to seem to know nothing about painting when
I come here."

Lilith had moved opposite to the picture of
"Queen Mab" on the easel.

"What do you think of this, Lord Falcon?" she asked; "does it please you?"

"Yes," replied Falcon, "it pleases me very much. It is an excellent portrait."

She looked keenly at him, but only said, as if she had seen no particular meaning in his speech—

"Papa is not supposed to be a portrait painter. Have you no other reason for liking it? Do you care for that kind of subject?"

"It has a certain attraction for me. Everything that takes us out of everyday life is pleasant. The world is so dull and wearisome in its monotony."

"The world dull?" said Vane. "I think it is a most amusing place. Do you find it dull, Miss von Waldheim?"

"Sometimes, horribly; there is no such thing as real excitement, nothing to stir all one's pulses and keep one's nerves on a continual strain. That would be something worth living for!" She made a gesture of impatience with her hands as she spoke, interlacing the fingers with a quick pressure, and her father, observing her with his keen watchful eyes, came up and said—

" Can you find me that sketch of the Hartz mountains? I think it will please Sir Harry more than any of these fanciful things."

She went to a portfolio, and drew out a sketch of a mountain view, with powerful effects of light and shade.

" How easily," said Vane, as she held up the sketch for inspection, " one can understand superstition being rife in such a place. I declare I can almost see the giant raftsman, Michael, lurking in that deep shadow beneath the trees."

" You have a quick imagination, Mr. Vane," said Lilith. " What a pity it is that papa cannot always secure such appreciative spectators for his pictures, is it not, Sir Harry?" she added with a malicious little smile.

"Just so," said Sir Harry.

Soon after this the young men took their leave. As they walked back Vane said to Falcon—

"What do you think of Miss von Waldheim now?"

"I have not your rapid power of forming opinions, Arthur," replied the other, "and I therefore reserve my decision. What do you think?"

"I think she is not a girl to know all at once, though I believe I exaggerated her singularity last night. One's feelings are excited by the glare and the music, the hum and the clatter, and the constant motion of a ball, and one is apt to see things in an ex-

travagant light. Don't you agree with me,
Harry ? "

" Quite so," said Sir Harry ; " there's
such a din and bustle going on all round you
that you don't know whether you're on your
head or your heels.   She is a queer little girl
though, that Miss von Waldheim, and so is
her father.   They get wrapped up in art and
one thing or another, and forget what goes
on in the world.   Why, I believe if you were
to ask old von Waldheim who was Prime
Minister he wouldn't know."

The three sank into silence after this.
Both Falcon's and Vane's reflections were
occupied with Lilith. Falcon, whose habit
of mind led him to consider all his impressions seriously, began to analyse his feelings
with regard to this girl, and before long
arrived at the conclusion that she had taken
a strong hold upon him ; he had seldom

before met any girl whom he had really cared
to see more than once; never one whom he
had desired to see a third time; and now
there was no doubt that he had left Mr. von
Waldheim's studio with a distinct intention
of returning to it again. He would not yet
acknowledge to himself that his heart was
touched by one of whom he had seen so little,
but he could not deny that such a state of
things was likely to arrive. He had com-
plained of the dulness and weariness of
external life, and here was a being who appeared to be neither dull nor wearisome, and
who on her side was vexed with the monotony
of the world. Then there certainly was something unusual in her nature, something fiery
and excitable which would always rouse a
man given too much to dreamy meditation
into action and life. Here he perceived that
his feelings were outrunning his reason and

wandering into dangerous ground, and so
forced them into another channel. His
cousin, meantime, wondered about many
things; wondered why he felt no inclination
to flirt with Lilith; wondered whether Falcon
did, and what Falcon would look like if he
condescended to flirt. Then he fell to envy-
ing his cousin a little for his power of con-
centration and self-mastery, and thinking
that if he himself had devoted to some one
study or art the time which he had spent in
cultivating many, in falling in and out of love,.
and in a hundred other fripperies, he might
have become such an one as Falcon. He
might just as well have hoped to add a cubit
to his stature by taking thought, but of this
fact he was ignorant. At Sir Harry's door
the three parted, Vane and Falcon going
away together, while Sir Harry went in.

"Well, Harry," said Lady Emmy, "how
did your visit go off?"

"Well enough," he replied. "I never care myself about von Waldheim's pictures, but I think Arthur and Falcon were pleased."

"Did Arthur flirt with Miss von Waldheim?"

"Not much; he doesn't seem to care about her, but I rather think Falcon does. He didn't say much, but I suspect he thought the more, like the monkeys."

"I hope you are mistaken," said Lady Emmy.

"Why? It strikes me it would be a very good thing. Falcon's sure to marry some one artistic if he marries at all, and you don't want him to remain single, I suppose. It seems to me that little girl would just suit him. She's rather odd herself, and would understand his odd ways. Do you know anything against her?"

"I know that she broke poor young Gordon's heart, and she is credited with numer-

ous feats of that kind. But that is nothing
—nothing, at least, to what I feel about her.
Women have a way of finding each other out
which happily or unhappily is not given to
men, and I do not like the look of Lilith von
Waldheim's eyes."

"She has very pretty eyes," said Sir
Harry; "perhaps that is why you abuse
them. Now you mention it, there is an odd
look about them, but I see no harm in that."

"I see much harm to come if Falcon
should care about her, and the worst part of
it is that there are no means of stopping it.
When he once makes up his mind he will do
so for ever, and he will allow no one to mend
or mar the process of making it up. You
will think I speak with exaggeration, but I
am confident that Falcon had better remain
single all his life than marry that girl."

"My dear Emmy," said Sir Harry, looking perturbed, "of course I think you take an exaggerated view. I think you often do, but then you're often right ; and if you really think so badly of the girl, I'm sorry I took Falcon there."

" He would have found other means of going if you had not done so. As for thinking badly of her, remember that I have nothing but my own thoughts to go upon, and pray never say a word of this to Falcon. Let us hope I have formed an unjust opinion."

When Lilith and her father were left alone he said to her—

" What do you think of our two new comers, little fairy ? "

" Mr. Vane seems very agreeable, and Lord Falcon very—thoughtful."

" Do you know what he was thinking about ? "

"No, papa," she said, climbing on to his knee and putting her arm round his neck; "but I suppose you do; you seem always to read people's minds."

"I can read yours enough to see that you know as well as I do what Lord Falcon was thinking about; but I will tell you, to make it yet more certain; he was thinking about you."

"Dear old papa! It is your fondness for me which makes you imagine everyone else must be fond of me. But do you really think it is so?" she added with charming inconsistency.

"I am certain of it; and do not think I want to scold you, my pet, if I warn you to give him no encouragement for which you cannot afterwards be accountable."

"Ah," she said with a little motion of vexation, "you are thinking of Frank

Gordon! It is unkind of you to remind me of that."

" Of him and of others. Do not be angry, fairy. I do not say that it was your fault. I do not believe it was."

" My fault! Do you think I meant to hurt him ? How could I tell that he cared for me like that ? "

" It is because you could not tell then that I wish you to use your experience now. Lord Falcon is a man who could ill bear such a blow."

" But papa, Lord Falcon has only seen me once."

" Lord Falcon is not as other men are altogether. But I do not want to put it into your vain little head that he is devoted to you already. I wish only to caution you."

" Yes, papa," she said gravely; " but you do not really think me vain, do you ? "

For all answer he kissed her, and with a half-sigh went to work at his painting again.

The Frank Gordon of whom both Lady Emmy and Mr. von Waldheim had spoken was a young man who was said to be of some promise, a vague phrase which is popular perhaps by force of its vagueness and consequent safety. No one can be accused of hypocrisy or want of judgment for saying than such an one has much promise when the performance to which the promise refers is left entirely in doubt. Young Gordon was, perhaps, not different from many other young men, in that he possessed very fair abilities, a tolerable industry in using them, and a brave and true heart. But he was different in this—that he possessed a vast capacity of loving, which he concentrated upon one object; and that object was Lilith. He had met her in London, as young people do meet;

had been fascinated by her, had sought her society continually, had imagined—whether with good reason or not—that his devotion to her was not unappreciated, had at last proposed to her, and been refused with some amazement and some expression of sorrow. There were those who said that she had never given him any real cause for hope, that he had no right to misinterpret what was merely friendship on her side and liking for his society and conversation; that he ought to have taken her fanciful nature and ways into account. There were also those who said that she had played fast and loose with him; that the manner in which she one day received him with sympathy and kindness and the next with a kind of trembling distrust, was enough to make any one form the conclusion which he had formed. Among these was Lady Emmy; but Frank

E

Gordon was rather a favourite of hers, and had confided all his sorrows to her. He had come to her soon after his rejection, and in the bitterness of his heart had said to her, "She played with me as a cat does with a mouse;" but the next moment he had wished to recall the words, and said that there was really no fault on her side, and that he alone was to blame for his folly in construing her words and actions according to his own desires, and not by the light of clear judgment. Lady Emmy's kind heart had been full of pity for the poor boy and of admiration for his chivalry in wishing to spare Lilith from reproach, and it may be that her view of the matter was prejudiced by her womanly sympathy. Certain it is that for a time he was, as she had said, broken-hearted, and had now fled from the scene of his disappointment to try to forget it in travel.

Lilith, as she posed herself in the pretty indolent attitude which her father had selected for Queen Mab, thought of him with a kind of pity which soon gave way to vexation at his having given her cause for regret. She could not understand why the credit or discredit of having filled his cup with misery should rest on her; it was not her fault if he had loved her and she had not cared to return his love. Then a feeling of gratification at possessing the power to stir men's hearts came over her, and she fell to thinking whether she did in truth possess that power over Lord Falcon's heart. For him she experienced a kind of respect which she did not remember to have known before: she felt as if in him she recognised something of her own restless, wayward nature, but felt also that in him, if it existed, it was subdued and quelled to impassiveness by a strong power of repression. Perhaps she thought such a faculty of bridling his own soul might be extended to hers, or perhaps her own might avail to break down its force; and at that thought she laughed with the little low laugh that was peculiar to her. Her father, hearing it, paused a moment in his work, to ask, "What is it, fairy?" and she answered him, "Nothing, dear papa; only some thoughts in my silly little head."

CHAPTER III.

A FEW nights after Falcon's first visit to Mr. von Waldheim's studio he went to the opera with Sir Harry Grey and Lady Emmy. She had dramatic and musical tastes which her husband shared to a certain extent, but not sufficiently to give her that delight of sympathy which she found in her brother's companionship. When the emotions are aroused by the magic of art the pleasure of excitement is doubled by the knowledge that it is shared by one whom we love and who is close to us.

When they witnessed together any great production of art, even if they interchanged no words, Lady Emmy knew that Falcon's feelings were stirred in the same kind, if not to the same degree as her own, and by the same influences. She looked forward to such occasions with almost a child's pleasure of anticipation. As they went to the opera on this night she said to her brother, "I am so glad it is the *Freischütz* to-night : Faure is so fine in ' Caspar.' "

" He is very fine," replied Falcon; " the grim recklessness which he preserves throughout the part is so different from the affected joviality of ordinary actors. The suppressed scorn of his victim, the despairing mirth as to himself which he infuses into the drinking song are wonderful. Of course I speak only of his acting now; about his singing there can be but one opinion."

" Yet," said Lady Emmy, " I have heard people say that they could not bear his voice."

" There's nothing wonderful in that,

Emmy," said Sir Harry; "if a thing is good you'll always find somebody to abuse it. If it's bad it isn't worth the trouble of picking holes in."

" A very just remark, Harry," said Falcon. " There are so many people, too, who go to the opera without caring one atom either for music or acting; it is the correct thing to do, and they do it, just in the same spirit which carries them to church on Sunday."

" Exactly so," said Sir Harry; " they come to look at each other. They'd be quite as pleased if there was a barrel organ playing tunes on the stage."

" I wonder," said Lady Emmy, " how many people in the house to-night will be interested in the wonderful acting of the incantation scene ? "

" That is, indeed, acting," said Falcon. " The terror which creeps over 'Caspar' gradually in spite of himself, which is always overmastered by fresh efforts of courage and purpose, can only be rendered as it is by a great artist."

" Yes," said Sir Harry, " that's quite true. You see that he doesn't care a bit for all the hobgoblins round him, and yet he's inclined to be in an awful fright all the time."

" Very well put, Harry," said Lady Emmy, with a laugh.

During the first act her expectations of en- joying the opera in concert with her brother were fully realized ; at every phrase of the music, every instance of the actors' or singers' skill which appealed to her fancy, she found a responsive look or pressure of a hand ready to assure her of Falcon's sym- pathy. At the conclusion she remained for a few seconds in silent admiration of the won- derful music of ' Caspar's ' song of triumph, and the wonderfully controlled fire with which it was interpreted; then she turned to communicate her impressions to Falcon, but he was gone.

"Looking for Falcon, little Emmy?" said her husband. "He's found an attraction on the opposite side. What do you think it is?"

"I know without looking," she replied. "Of course it is sure to be Lilith von Wald-heim." And looking at the boxes on the other side she saw that in fact her brother was talking to Lilith in a box occupied by her, her father, and Arthur Vane. "My poor boy!" said Lady Emmy, regretfully, as she noted the earnestness which appeared in his face.

"Come, don't be so desponding, Emmy," said her husband. "Remember you told me the other day that you had nothing to make you really think ill of her."

"I cannot help it, dear," she said. "I should be anxious about Falcon, I believe, even if I knew he were devoting himself to an angel; and however little I know about Lilith von Waldheim, I am sure she does not come under that head."

Falcon had greeted the von Waldheims with more warmth than he generally put into the ordinary courtesies of life.

"This is an unexpected pleasure," he had said. "I did not know that you affected the opera."

"Nor do we often," said Mr. von Waldheim; "but we are both very fond of this opera, and Mr. Vane kindly offered us these places this afternoon."

"I would have let you know," said Vane to Falcon, in whose face he fancied there was a shade of displeasure; "but I only got the box just in time to go round to Mr. von Waldheim."

"You are fond of this music?" said Falcon to Lilith.

"I am fond of this opera. I believe I like anything that has to do with *diablerie*," she replied, with a slight, quick turn of her head and a confiding look, as if she were telling him something which she would not tell to any one else. "You are very musical, are you not?"

"I love music."

"What instrument do you play? All? Tell me."

"I can play several, but there are few that interest me much singly. Practically, the piano answers one's purposes better than anything else."

"The piano—yes," she said; "but there is a want of strength sometimes in the piano. If I were a musician, I think I would like nothing so much as to lead an orchestra, to sway all those minds and fingers at once with the motion of your hand, to be absolute in rule over all that collected skill and power down there—that would be splendid! Next to that, I think I would play the organ; there is such depth and grandeur in it. Do you play it, Lord Falcon?"

"Whenever I get a chance. At least, that is not quite true, for I have had one chance which I have neglected for a long time. There is an old organ at my house in the country which I have never touched; but for that there are some reasons."

"Reasons! I should think there were!" cried Vane, who had heard Falcon's last few words. "There are such stories about"—

His sentence was interrupted by his cousin laying a significant grip, unseen by the others, on his arm, and faltering for a moment, he finished it in these words—

"I mean I should think the pipes are all tumbling to pieces by this time."

"You have an old house?" said Lilith to Falcon. "How interesting that must be! Are not those two ladies to whom you are bowing Mrs. Norman and Miss Norman? Are you going down to see them?"

"No," said he in a low voice; "I prefer staying where I am."

She smiled as a person who had just done a good action might smile, and at that moment the curtain rose upon the incantation scene. Then followed that fine effort of the actor's art, of which Falcon and his sister had spoken. The player's power over himself was communicated to the spectators; their minds followed in the track of his until the wild horrors indicated on the stage acquired a real importance, and Vane's vivid sensibilities were so excited that, although he knew the scene by heart, it became a question of actual moment to him whether "Caspar's" courage would give way under the accumulation of terrors which attacked it. He gave a sigh of mingled admiration and relief when, at last, standing with outstretched arms, surrounded with a grim glory of hellish fires, the hunter, as he cast the seventh bullet, pronounced in desperate triumph the fatal "Sette." Lilith had manifested even more interest and excitement: her eyes glittered, her colour came and went, and as the curtain fell she clutched her father's arm as if to seek some support or outlet for her emotion. He laid his hand on her's quietly, and said,

"It is a wonderful power, to endow the tricks of the stage-carpenter with life, to carry one away as one sits here, into the regions of wild romance."

"Yes," said Vane, "it must be splendid to act when one can act like that."

"Splendid to act!" repeated Lilith, "how much more splendid it would be to do!"

Falcon looked at her seriously. Vane said, " I am afraid there is little opportunity for that, Miss von Waldheim; the wood demons have had their day; civilisation has driven them from their haunts; and even if they were there, the courage to call them up might be wanting."

" I do not think it would be wanting in Miss von Waldheim," said Falcon, with an inclination of his head to her.

" I am afraid it would not," said her father abstractedly.

Soon after this Falcon rejoined his sister and brother-in-law, not before he had made arrangements for going soon to see how Mr. von Waldheim's picture was getting on.

Falcon with his sister and Sir Harry drove home in a silence which was only broken by Sir Harry observing in his cheerful tones, " A very attractive little girl, that Miss von

Waldheim. You seem to find lots to say to her, Falcon. Now, I never can tell what to talk to her about; I can't make up my mind whether she's laughing at me or not." The only reply he received to this remark was a warning look from his wife. Falcon seemed lost in abstraction, and did not display any consciousness of what had been said.

Lady Emmy observed him with some anxiety, and when he said good-night, looked closely at him with her kind grey eyes, and said, "Cecil, dear, remember what I said to you : do take care what you are about."

He replied : " Dear little Emmy, don't you think I am old enough to take care of myself?" and then walked on to his club, where he encountered Vane, who received him with " Well, Falcon, how did you like the opera to-night ?"

" I liked it much ; it is a fine opera, and

very dramatic; it appeals both to eye and ear."

"Ille mi par esse deo videtur,
Ille si fas est superare divos
Qui sedens adversus identidem te
Spectat et audit,
Dulce ridentem."

quoted Vane, mischievously.

"I was speaking of the opera," answered Falcon, with a slight smile.

"And thinking of it? Answer me now the question I asked you some time ago—what do you think about Miss von Waldheim?"

"I told you when you asked me, that I do not form my opinions quickly; but I will tell you this much now; I think a good deal about her."

"So!" said Vane. "And how does the music get on? Have you begun the oratorio that is to astonish the world yet?"

F

"I will tell you another thing," said Falcon, "I have not written a bar for a week."

"Oh!" replied Vane, "I have got an answer to my first question now."

Falcon, as he walked home that night, bent his thoughts in the direction which for some time past they had been accustomed to follow. He now began to recognise plainly the fact that Lilith von Waldheim had become the centre of his feelings and reflections. He had gone on carefully observing her, thinking over her, ever since the first occasion of their meeting; he had intended to wait and see whether the impression made upon him then was in truth of that strength which he was disposed to assign to it, or whether he at last had fallen by chance into that way of transient emotions which his Cousin Arthur had followed for so long. But this waiting upon the passions, this endeavour to separate as it were one's identity from one's emotions, is a dangerous feat to attempt. While Falcon had thought to watch the current of his feelings from a safe post of observation, and stem it if need be, he had been swept down by it, and he now perceived that it would task his strength severely to get out of the stream in which he was plunged; and thinking over matters, he came to the conclusion that on the whole he did not want to get out of it; it was good to go down yet further with the stream, and reach perhaps its ultimate goal, whether that should prove a quiet lake or a stormy sea. Having resolved his doubts, and made up his mind thus far, he took to his music, and succeeded in composing a piece of solemn recitative tolerably to his own satisfaction.

Vane's reflections as he walked home were

of a vaguer kind. Scenes from the opera mingled with recollections of Lilith flitted across his mind. He had begun to like her much, and thought she had been most unjustly and hardly spoken of by those who found fault with her. She was not to be blamed if she had a caressing kind of manner; it was stupid of young men to think it was meant for them alone; why he, who was always ready to plunge deep into a flirtation had never misinterpreted it. She was clever too, and seemed to have an individuality and a will of her own, which it was a relief to meet with in these dead-level days. He could imagine making a friend of such a woman. Then he wondered if he was right in thinking that Falcon was becoming seriously attached to her—it certainly looked rather like it. If it was so, and if it resulted, as it well might, in a marriage, why then it would probably turn out very well, and no one would be more glad of it than himself. Such was the train of Vane's thoughts, and such he fancied was their conclusion.

The next week or two, in the course of which the two young men met several times at Mr. von Waldheim's studio, and took part in visits with him and his daughter to plays and picture galleries, confirmed Falcon in his growing devotion to Lilith, while to Vane she continued to appear different from other girls, in that she commanded his steady regard.

Lady Emmy watched what was going on with anxiety, while Sir Harry was at one time actuated by his somewhat careless good-nature to assist Falcon in arranging meetings with the von Waldheims, at another overcome with remorse at seeing the trouble which the state of affairs gave to his wife.

It was some three weeks after that visit to the opera which has been recorded, that the two young men met at the painter's studio for the ostensible purpose of looking at the " Queen Mab " picture before it received the final touches from his hands.

They and Mr. von Waldheim stood in front of the picture, the artist with the air of a man, on the whole, well content with what he had done, but yet careful and thoughtful about it. Vane assumed the critic, looked at it with eyes shaded with his hands, walked a little way from it, and then returned to his former place with a wise shake of the head. Falcon's aspect was singularly impassive. Lilith flitted about around them as they looked, with the grace and noiselessness of a cat, while her eyes as they wandered from Vane to Falcon and from Falcon to Vane shone with glee.

"Well," said Mr. von Waldheim, after

some time, bending his brows at Vane, "what do you think of it? what suggestions have you to make?"

"Only one of any importance," replied Vane, "and even if you should think that worthy of attention, it may be too late to act upon it. There is an impatient expression on ' Queen Mab's ' face which seems to me out of keeping, out of character, with the subject. She is surrounded by an adoring court, and has every reason to be well content. Why should she have that restless, craving look?"

"Ah, bah!" replied the artist. "You must not judge her by too high a standard; mortal heads may be uneasy under a crown, and restless with all the appearance of happiness, and fairies are not a bit more accountable for their actions than mortals. Are they, Lilith?" he said, turning to her.

"No, indeed, papa," she answered, pressing her hand on his arm, and nestling her head on his shoulder, while she looked softly up into his eyes. He looked down at her with an expression half delighted, half regretful.

" Come, Mr. Vane," he said, as he gently disengaged himself from her, " will you give me your opinion on the arrangement of the light in this corner? You will see it is the same kind of effect that I have got in this large picture of the ' Brocken.' " He walked up to the picture over the mantelpiece, whither Vane followed him; while Falcon continued to gaze at " Queen Mab," and Lilith to gaze at Falcon.

" Lord Falcon," she said presently, " have you any objections to make? " He turned, and as he looked at her the impassibility of his expression suddenly broke up and softened.

" Only one objection," he said, with grave

deliberation, "it does not do justice to the original."

Lilith made no answer to this, save by her low-toned laugh, which might have almost any interpretation, according to the frame of mind of the person to whom it was addressed; and at this moment there came a sudden cry from Vane, and a noise of something falling.

One stride brought Falcon to the aid of his cousin. The large picture at which he and the artist were looking had suddenly broken away from its fastenings, and dropped, with all its weight, towards Mr. von Wald- heim, on whose head it must have fallen had not Vane interfered, with dexterous agility, and broken its fall with his arm. Falcon helped him to lower the picture gradually, while Lilith rushed to her father and inquired anxiously, "Are you hurt, papa?" to which he replied, "No, but I might have been killed but for Mr. Vane." Then turning to Vane, she said, "How can I thank you enough, dear Mr. Vane, for saving papa?" thrust out both her little hands and clasped his in them. She looked full into his eyes, and held his hands for some moments in hers, and then cried with quick sympathy, "Your hand is shaking dreadfully—you are hurt?"

"No, no," said Vane, "it is nothing, it is only the effect of a sudden strain—I am not hurt; indeed, I assure you, I am not hurt."

He pressed her hands for an instant as he spoke, as though to convey more strongly this assurance, and his delight at her father's safety.

Soon after this incident Vane, who had an engagement, took his departure; and Lilith presently going out of the room to give directions to a servant, Falcon was left alone with Mr. von Waldheim. His thoughts and feel-

ings had been gradually shaping themselves
into a final form for some days past, and now
he gave them expression in words.

He stood up and faced the painter, looking,
with his dignified bearing, his well cut
features, and the generous, fearless expression in his clear, deep eyes, like one of
Titian's portraits.

"Mr. von Waldheim," said Falcon, "I
am going to ask you a very serious thing."

The painter, with as much dignity of
aspect, though of a different kind, bowed his
head in token of readiness to listen, and knit
his brows together as if to see more clearly
from under their shelter.

"I ask you," went on Falcon, "to do for
me the utmost that you can do for any man:
I ask you to deliver up to my keeping that
which must be more precious to you than
anything on earth: to entrust me with the

life and happiness of your daughter—if she will come to me. Of my love for her, of the joy that will enter into my life if I am so happy as to be the guardian of hers, I think I need hardly speak."

"Lord Falcon," replied Mr. von Wald-heim, after a short pause, "I do not know the man whom I would so willingly—so gladly, let me say—see Lilith's husband as yourself. You have spoken truly in saying that she is more precious to me than any-thing on earth. I am always anxious for her; I think I always shall be anxious for her, even if she is in the keeping of one whom I esteem so highly as I do you. She is unlike other girls, poor child! Since she was four years old she has had no mother. But all this is wandering from the matter in hand. I have told you what I think as to that myself; it is more important to know

what Lilith thinks. If she thinks with me —
well; if not let me assure you that I shall
be grieved. I cannot pretend to interpret
her feelings to you in any way; and if I
could I doubt not you would rather hear
them explained by herself. If you will wait
here I will ask her to come to you."

The two men, neither of whom was given
to much display of emotion, interchanged a
grip of the hand, and Falcon was left alone.

As has been said, he had sifted and
examined his mind thoroughly before he had
spoken; he had arrived at the sure decision
that if he gained that which he asked for he
would gain the greatest happiness that life
could give him; on the other hand, if it
should be denied to him, he must bear the
denial without flinching. Therefore, however quickly his heart might have been beat-
ing, with whatever violence doubts and fears

and hopes might have been rushing and chasing each other through his brain, he preserved a calm attitude and exterior, which he disturbed only by one quick, eager step forward as Lilith entered the room.

She came in with a step slower than her ordinary one, and her head was bent towards the ground; but her eyes shone with the same triumphant light which had been in them on the first occasion of her meeting Falcon in this room.

" You will have heard from your father, Miss von Waldheim," Falcon began, as soon as they were near to each other, " of the purpose with which I have sought this interview. Since first I met you—how long ago that was I can hardly tell, for of late I have kept count of time only by your presence or absence—I have thought of little else but you. Happiness has been since then found

nowhere for me save in the sound of your
voice, the light of your eyes, the touch of
your hand. I can never love anyone else as
I love you. I have come here to-day to ask
you if you can make that happiness mine for
ever; if you will be my wife."   .
    He spoke steadily and slowly, but with a
passionate anxiety which was not the less
evident because it was repressed; he stood
now with his hands clasped together in front
of him, looking down at Lilith with grave,
waiting eyes. She had raised her head but
once during his speech, to dart at him a swift
look. "What a noble bearing," she thought,
as she lowered her glance again; "what a
strength of will! what a power of self-command!" In the brief interval during which
she stood silent and motionless after his last
words, many thoughts and feelings passed in
swift succession through her mind; a joy that

this moment had come which she had long ago determined should come; a triumphant delight in her power over such a man as Lord Falcon; a passing remembrance of Arthur Vane, and a wonder as to what his feelings would be when he heard of this; then came for an instant a vague feeling of dread, at what—whether at Falcon or at herself, or at what she was about to do, she could not tell; and the next moment she looked up at him with the confiding, tender smile which was one of her charms, and held out her hand to him, saying—

"I should love of all things to make you happy, and if you think that will make you happy, I will be your wife."

He seized her hand, and kissed it passion- ately, and then clasped her in a close embrace.

"If I think!" he cried. "My darling,

what happiness in the whole world can there be like mine now? Till this moment I never knew how bright the world was."

" Not even when you listened to great music?" she asked playfully.

" Sweetest, there is more music for me now in one word from your lips," he replied, " than in all the operas, all the sonatas which the world contains."

He led her to one of the large chairs which stood about the room, and sat down in a lower one by her side, holding her hand and looking up into her face. She looked at him as if in doubt or perplexity for a moment, and then a lost, far-away expression came into her eyes, seeing which he said—

" Of what are you thinking, dear?"

" I don't quite know," she answered with a little start; " but I fancy I was thinking that you have known me a very short time."

G

"Love takes no thought of time," he answered.

"And I do not think you know me very well," she went on, paying no attention to his reply.

"I know that I love you very well."

"For that reason you think too well of me; people often do. I am neither so good nor so clever as you think me; and I feel as if I ought to tell you that. It is true, indeed it is."

Falcon was enchanted with her frankness.

"Darling," he said, "you must let me be judge as to that. I know you better than you know yourself."

"I do not think any one knows me well. I do not know myself—so perhaps it may be that you do know me better. You do love me, don't you?" she answered with a quick change of voice.

"With my whole being," he replied passionately.

At this moment Mr. von Waldheim's step was heard outside the door, and he, entering the room, saw by Falcon's expression what answer Lilith had given him.

"I see," he said as he came towards them. "My fairy, I congratulate you on your choice. Lord Falcon, I need not repeat what I have already said to you," and once again he pressed Falcon's hand warmly.

It was now late in the afternoon, and Falcon took his leave till the next day. As he went he stooped to caress Lilith's great Persian cat, which lay in his usual place on the rug.

"Take care!" cried Lilith; "he will bite and scratch you; he is apt to scratch at every one but me, and he is cross to-day."

She ran forward to intercept his hand, but it was too late; the cat had torn it already, and she caught it only in time to transfer to her own tiny fingers some of the blood-stain which the animal's claws left on Falcon's hand. She gave a little shudder as she looked at the mark.   Falcon, seeing it, said—

"A bad omen ; but we will laugh omens to scorn."

The artist, however, frowned, and said in harsh tones—

"You should keep your pets in better order, Lilith."

CHAPTER IV.

WHILE all this was taking place at Mr. von Waldheim's studio, Arthur Vane had gone to see Lady Emmy, and had conveyed to her the intelligence that he had left her brother alone at the studio, and that he fancied Falcon was getting to think more and more seriously of the artist's daughter. Lady Emmy said very little at the time, but when Vane had gone and her husband came in, she said to him—

"Harry, things are going on just as I feared they would with my boy; he is getting more and more infatuated with Lilith von Waldheim, and I would give my right hand to stop it."

" Well, dear," said Sir Harry, " I'm afraid

that wouldn't do much good; besides, I
might object."

" This is no laughing matter, really, dear
Harry," said she. " I feel so certain that
mischief will come of it if he should go so far
as to propose to her."

" What? do you mean she'll reject him,
and he'll be miserable ? "

" No, no ; better he should be miserable
for years ; of course she will accept him."

" Just so, of course she will," said Sir
Harry. " It's a great chance for her ; she
would like to be Lady Falcon, I am sure.
Besides, I think she likes him."

" Who can tell what her likes and dislikes
may be ?   Who can read the secret of her
unfathomable eyes ? "

" It seems to me, Emmy, that you've got
a kind of craze about her eyes. But if you
really take it so much to heart—and, after

all, you know Falcon a great deal better than any one else does—can't something be done?"

"What can be done? What would make Falcon alter one iota of his intention when he has made it, as I fear he has? Even if I could tell him more about Lilith von Waldheim than I can, would he heed it coming from me? He would only set it down as over anxiety for him, mixed, perhaps, with a spice of woman's jealousy."

"Just so, that's very true," said Sir Harry, who was here struck with a sudden inspiration which he acted upon that evening by going to see Arthur Vane. Having arrived at his rooms, and found him at home, he walked up and down in a nervous manner for a space, while Vane waited in amusement, knowing from these signs that some grave communication would follow. Presently Sir

Harry gave utterance to that which was brewing in his mind.

"Have you been at old von Waldheim's often lately with Falcon?" he asked.

"Yes, tolerably often," replied Vane.

"And—a—what do you think about him and Miss von Waldheim?"

"I think she has made a very strong impression on him."

"Ah, just so!" said Sir Harry. "Now, I'm not going to say a word against that little girl. She's a friend of yours, I believe; and, indeed, I haven't got a word to say. Emmy says she was a terrible flirt once, and if she was, I don't see that that was any crime; besides, women always say those things of each other. But don't you think that"—

Here Sir Harry's eloquence failed him, and he stopped dead short.

"Well?" said Vane, rather enjoying the other's perplexity.

"Well—what I mean is, that it never could be a suitable match for Falcon. He ought to marry somebody of his own *monde*, like Miss Norman, for instance: somebody with some ideas of convention, to tame down his odd ways. Now you know, if he is to marry Miss von Waldheim, between them both they'll be turning the world upside down."

"There is some truth in that, no doubt," said Vane, thoughtfully. "But what is to be done?"

"Just what Emmy said," replied Sir Harry, with a self-satisfied chuckle. "I didn't say anything to her, but I thought the thing to be done was to come and talk to you. If anybody can put the thing before Falcon in some light like that, you can."

"I can hardly tell him that Miss von Waldheim and he would upset the world."

"Of course not—of course not; but you might hint something about wisdom, and prudence, and reflection. He's devoted to you, and more likely to listen to you than to any one else."

Vane paused in thought a little, and then said—

"Well, I will do what I can; but that, I am sure, will not be much."

"Oh, I am sure Falcon will listen to anything you say."

"And never act upon it. However, I will try."

It was with considerable relief that Sir Harry took his departure, being convinced that he had done much to prevent that occurrence which his wife so much dreaded. Vane, as has been seen, undertook the unusual

task demanded of him with a readiness somewhat singular under the circumstances. He
said not a word in praise of Lilith, with whom
he certainly was now on terms of friendship.
He acceded quietly to all that Sir Harry
advanced against her making a fit wife for
Falcon. There was, indeed, a considerable
portion of truth in this, as he could not deny;
yet he wondered, after Sir Harry had gone,
why he had not spoken to him of her clever-
ness and brightness, and the many good
qualities which he discerned in her. Finally,
he laid his silence to the account of the deep
interest which he took in Falcon's welfare.
But Vane was not a very correct interpreter
of his own feelings. However, he resolved
to see his cousin, and beg him to reflect
before he took any important step.

"Of course he will reflect without my
asking him," said Arthur, to himself; "still

I may put the thing to him in a fresh light, and anyhow I shall have done no harm, and perhaps gratified Emmy."

Next morning, accordingly, Vane called upon Falcon, and went straight to his object.

"Much as you dislike interference," he said, "I have come to interfere with you for once. I have observed for a long time past, as you are aware, a growing inclination on your part for Miss von Waldheim. I know that you are so likely to have thought over everything, studied everything about her, much more closely and keenly than I could with my less steady nature, that I will say only this to you. Pray think yet a little more— pray study yet a little more—before you take any decisive step. Come away—to the country or the Continent—with me, if you will, for a week or two, and see whether you are still in the same mind. Of course I know that while I make and unmake my mind fifty times, you make up yours once and for all; but I do not forget that in speaking thus. The wisest of us may be mistaken as to our own hearts; and your welfare is so dear to all of us, that I have felt urged to say this. Knowing why I have said it you will forgive me for saying it."

"I forgive you, my dear Arthur, and I thank you," said Falcon; "but you are too late. I proposed to Lilith, and was accepted, yesterday. I was about to come and ask for your congratulations when you arrived just now."

Vane started back, and opened his mouth with surprise. Then he advanced to Falcon and shook him warmly by the hand.

"My dear Falcon, I do congratulate you heartily," he said.

He experienced a curious feeling as he

spoke the words. He felt much surprise at Falcon's quickness of action, much pleasure at the prospect of his happiness, which he trusted would be established in spite of Lady Emmy's forebodings.

Mingled with these feelings, however, was a tinge of another feeling, to which, had he not been certain that what he himself felt for Lilith was mere friendship, he would have been inclined to give the name of regret, or even of something more violent. As it was, he dismissed it as he had a way of doing with transient impressions which troubled him. After all, it might be a shade of selfish regret at the inevitable loss, to some extent, of the society of two friends, which he must now put up with.

Not many weeks after this Lord Falcon and Lilith were married, and went for a tour on the Continent.

CHAPTER V.

On their return from foreign travel, the Earl and Countess came to take up their residence at Falcontree Hall. The house stands on a slight eminence at the head of a small village, which slopes down a hill to the sea in one of the most remote parts of the English coast.

There, as yet, no railway engine has screamed its discordant and dangerous message of progress and civilization; and there the inhabitants are distinguished by a simplicity of mind, and a grand manner resulting from that simplicity, which they would perhaps lose were they nearer to the turmoil of the world. There is a kindly community of feeling among them which is rarely found in collected humanity. Many of them have sailed in trading ships to far corners of the earth, to Japan, to America, to Australia, all of which places are included by that part of the population which remains at home under the generic term of " out foreign."

But however many, however long, may be those voyages, the voyagers return from them to Falcontree village as to a home, and are greeted by their old friends and companions as being members of the same family, on excellent terms with each other—wherein they differ from some families. They are far from want of interest in the doings of mankind, but however important may be the wars or rumours of wars which rack statesmen's brains and stir the pulses of Europe, it cannot be denied that to the natives of this village the results of the fishing have a much nearer importance.

They are not deeply troubled by the calamities which may affect thousands in the capital, but when sorrow comes to one of themselves, it is in a measure the sorrow of all. For these advantages, if they are advantages, there must be some counter-weight. The want of intimate acquaintance with the movement of the times accounts for the presence among the villagers of certain habits of mind once common to humanity at large, now exploded for the most part, save in places where the exploding influence of science has not yet brought its force to bear. Among such habits is that of superstitious belief, and for the exercise of this no better object could be found than Falcontree Hall. The house had been, until the return of Lord Falcon and his wife, practically uninhabited since the latter part of the seventeenth century, when another Lord Falcon had lived

H

there for a time with his wife, and had disappeared, leaving behind him a weird memento, in the shape of a picture, which he caused to be hung in the organ-room.

This room, it should be said, is on the right hand as one enters the hall. The hall doors look out on a terrace studded with flower-beds, and bounded by a low wall wherein is a wicket-gate, whence a narrow and precipitous path leads down through wooded cliffs to the sea. As to the reasons which induced that Lord Falcon who possessed the house at the time spoken of to leave it suddenly, there were many rumours; but the facts, which were generally supposed to affect in some way the honour of the family, had been so carefully hushed up by him that even at the time no one could say how much truth lay in the many stories set afloat to account for his proceedings, and naturally through the lapse of years these tales were credited with less and less certainty. They had blended, however, at length into one form more or less definite, which depended for its truth as much upon the picture in the organ-room as upon anything else. It was supposed that there had been some quarrel between Lord Falcon and his wife; that he had separated from her, under what circumstances precisely no one pretended to determine; that unable to bear the associations of life in England, he had gone over to Holland, where he learnt as a pastime or a distraction the art of painting. There he painted the picture which hung in the organ-room; once more he returned to Falcontree Hall to place it on the wall; and then retired again to the Low Countries, where he died. The picture was supposed to represent more or less accurately the closing

scene of his married life, an unhappy drama
enough if it did so close. The background
shows the room wherein the picture hangs
seen by moonlight; an old oak-panelled room,
to which there clung even in later times a
faint fragrance of bygone days; a remi-
niscence of the past seemed to float about
its walls, an atmosphere of lace and ruffles,
of heavy silks and drooping curls, a far-off
echo from the rustle of flirting fans and the
clank of jealous swords. The ghosts of
Cavaliers and Court ladies seemed to bow and
bridle in its dark corners. In the foreground
of the painting are three figures, two men
and a woman habited in the costume which
has been rendered familiar through Lely's
and Kneller's portraits. One of the male
figures was ascertained by reference to con-
temporary pictures to be a portrait of Lord
Falcon; he stands with a drawn and blood-

stained sword over the other, writhing in his death-agony on the ground. The woman, probably intended for Lady Falcon, stands a little back, in an attitude indicating a mingled triumph and despair. Her hands are stretched towards the dying man, presumably her lover, in a gesture part caressing, part shrinking ; and on her face is an expression difficult to describe, so much is there in it of horror, so much also of a fierce joy. This was strange, and there was also something strange in the look of the dying man, whose eyes, expressing all the terror and remorse that can be crowded into a man's last moments, were turned, not to Lord Falcon, not to the injured husband who had just dealt him his death-blow—a well-merited punishment, it may be, for his crime—but to Lady Falcon, the partner of that crime. Had they been turned to her in love, in pity, even in reproach, that direction might have been easily understood, might well have been the last direction in which his heart might have guided them : but they were not so turned. They looked towards her with an expression of bitter, hopeless misery, of vague and sudden horror, such as may be seen on the face of a man who struggles with some over-powering nightmare, which chills his blood and draws cold drops of sweat to his brow,. and who wakes to find his vision true. Such a look might have been seen on his face had the thrust that let out his life come from the hands of the woman whom he had loved, and who had loved him, instead of from the hands of the man whom he had dishonoured. The only explanation offered for this peculiarity was in one of the least credited rumours current concerning the event, according to which Lady Falcon, either by an impulse of

weariness or despair, or by some unhappy
mischance, had herself betrayed her lover
to her husband's vengeance. Whatever the
details of the fact might be, there was no
doubt that it led to Lord Falcon's separa-
tion from his wife, and to his living and
dying abroad. Nor was there any doubt
that it led also to the attaching of an ill-
repute to the room in which the picture
hung. There were stories, disregarded at
first as the idle tales of idle servants who
had nothing better to do than to invent
them, of mysterious sounds coming from
the organ-room, of stately marches and
heart-rending symphonies, played by some
invisible hand, issuing from the unused key-
boards. The music, it was said, by its
wondrous power and beauty drew the whole
household to listen to it with hushed voices
and hardly-drawn breath, until the unseen

fingers struck some notes so penetrating, so appalling in their discord, that by a common impulse those who heard them gazed on one another in dumb horror, as though they had listened to the voice of a fiend, and parted in affright. The diabolical harshness of the closing notes seemed to the guilty to recall and bring to light crimes that they had long thought buried out of sight, forgotten even by themselves; to the innocent, it opened a view of horrors which until then they had never imagined, which had been until then beyond or below their range of vision, from the suggestion of which they fled immediately, hoping vainly to escape even its remembrance. This ghastly music, as the story went, had been heard once by the successor of that unfortunate Earl who was supposed to have avenged his slain honour by the slaying of its destroyer, and

so soon as he had heard it he set his seal
on the organ-room whence it came, shut up
the house, and spent the rest of his life
far from his ancestral home. And partly
from indolence, partly from habit, partly
because Falcontree was a place wherein
there was but little excitement to be found,
his successors had in a great measure followed his example, coming down only at
rare intervals and for short periods to the
Hall, and never disturbing the seal set on
that room which was said to have been
the scene of a fearful tragedy. Thus the
village of Falcontree, where, as has been
said, even in the nineteenth century, when
superstition, except it take the form of
spiritualism or thought-reading, is much dis-
credited, some superstition lingers, was not
a little disturbed at the intelligence which
reached them that Lord Falcon and his

young wife intended to re-open and reside in what the inhabitants regarded as an accursed house.

The terror of the Hall's grim story, dim and vague though it was through lapse of time, hung over them still. The opening of the house was bad enough, but when orders arrived that the seal of the organ-room should be broken, the picture cleaned, and the organ restored, for which latter purposes Lord Falcon had men, regarded by the natives as agents of evil, sent down from London, a universal shudder ran through the village, from the house that touched the manorial woods on the top of the hill to that which opened straight on the sea-beach at the bottom.

During the process of restoration and addition the creaking pedals and rusty pipes of the organ gave out many a groan and shrieking note, as of anguish at being awaked to remembrance, which never failed to make the old housekeeper's cheek pale and her step falter, while she murmured a prayer of preservation from evil.

She and the gardener, who had grown grey in tending the flowers which were cared for only by him, were agreed upon this point.

" I can't scarcely think it's true now, Mrs. Thornton," would Gillie, the gardener, say to her, " what they were telling down along, that the young Lord's going to open the organ-room again. Why, old Howard tells as he's heard the ghost many a time when he's been coming through the grounds after night-fall, and he's so true a man as ever I see."

And Mrs. Thornton, bending graciously from her lofty respectability to old Gillie, privileged by age and long service to address her on equal terms, would reply—

"I do hope, Mr. Gillie, as it mayn't be true. I read in the paper the other day that the young Lord's on his way home, so I may expect a letter with orders from him before long. But won't you please to come in and take a glass of wine?"

And then the two would discuss together the evil results that would follow the young Lord's rash act, dwelling on all the ghostly stories they could find in their memories with delighted horror, until they saw phantoms in every shadow of Mrs. Thornton's room, and heard the sound of the organ in every gust of the sea-breeze.

Surely, they agreed, such a thing as the young Lord was about to do was no less than a direct temptation of Providence; and Providence, they implied, would not be slow in yielding to that temptation. But Falcon, like Gallio, cared for none of these things.

He laughed himself in his stately way at the ideas of horror attaching to Falcontree Hall, but he tried in vain to induce his housekeeper and tenants to sympathise with his laugh. He had chosen to reside for some time at Falcontree Hall for several reasons, not the least powerful among which was the desire to banish the superstitious awe with which it was invested.

Besides this, he wished to be in some place of picturesque associations, where he could indulge his musical broodings and give, as he hoped, completion and lasting life to the oratorio already begun. Also he thought the fresh soft air from the sea would be good for Lilith, who seemed somewhat worn and wearied by the fatigue and excitement of their travels.

Their tour had been successful and pleasant; he had loved her at its conclusion better, if that were possible, than before. Her wayward nature, which had come out with some strength on one or two occasions, had but served to endear her to him, both by the variety which it gave to her attractions, and by the strength of will which he thought he detected underneath it.

She had many moods, no doubt, but in all of them Falcon adored her equally; whether she smiled joyously at him and petted him with childlike caresses, or whether she frowned, and pouted, and rewarded all his efforts to please her with hard words, spoken half in jest, half in earnest, he was at all moments ready to do her bidding. It was certainly excusable in him that he should like to watch her admiringly as she flitted from room to room of the old house when they came down to Falcontree Hall.

All the graceful lightness of her nature, all the charm of her quick girlish merriment

came to the surface as she tripped rapidly
from chamber to chamber while Falcon kept
pace with her in his long stride. She peeped
into all the dark corners, opened all the doors
which had not for years been touched by
so light a hand, not perhaps since the hand
of the unhappy lady who figured in the
picture had been laid upon them.

She explored all the ancient recesses of
the house with the fresh thoughtless delight
of a child who is pleased with a new toy,
making all sorts of pretty, laughing com-
ments as she went. But when they reached
the organ-room, and trod the planks on which
many years ago a terrible death scene had
been enacted, a cloud seemed to come over
her mirth; her laughter ceased, and her
mouth drooped at the corners, as she stood
looking round her with a perplexed, pained
expression, and said presently—

"Falcon! do not laugh at me; you know

my superstitious nature, the sympathy which
I have with what I call the supernatural,
in spite of your contempt; that sympathy
tells me that there is something evil in this
room."

Falcon certainly had no such sympathy;
yet knowing the tendency of his wife's mind
to mystic imaginations and terrors, he had
carefully hidden from her the fact that any
story of ghostly import belonged to Falcontree Hall. In spite of himself, in spite of
the habit of thought which led him to look
upon such tendencies in most cases with
contempt—in the case of Lady Falcon with
affectionate pity—he was disagreeably surprised, even shocked, at the rapidity with
which she had fallen into the spirit of superstition which seemed to hover darkly about
the house.

He had disliked much the task of conceal-

ing from her the story of the Hall, which he
had regarded as a deception necessary in
order to prevent the unpleasant associations
of the place from working upon her nerves;
now he feared for a moment that the deception might in the end prove useless. But his
will, trained by long custom, exerted itself
to dispel this transient uneasiness, and he
replied to her with his kind, grave smile—

"What should there be evil in the room,
little kitten? Not you or I, surely. It has
not been opened for long, and the dust of I
know not how many years has accumulated
in it, and perhaps clings to it, and makes it
noxious still. But when the windows have
been left open for a few more days all that
will pass off, and it will be a pleasant habit-
able room enough."

While Falcon spoke thus, and threw the
windows wide open, his wife's attention had

I

been caught by the picture, and as he looked round he saw her gazing at it intently, with a strange look of fascination and dislike, of disgust and attraction, expressed in her wide steady eyes, in her parted lips, and in her frowning brow.

"Falcon!" she said, "what is this picture? Has it not a story, a dark story attached to it? I am sure it has. There is a fascination and a horror about it. It is the kind of picture that papa might have done, only he would never have painted anything with so little relief in it. I am certain it has a history. What is it?"

"A history, my pet?" replied Falcon, whose recent sense of uneasiness began to return to him. "What history should there be? It was painted, hung up, grew dirty, has been cleaned. What is there in that which might not be the history of all pictures that have been painted since the world began ? "

" No, no, no ! " she cried, tapping her foot impatiently upon the ground. " This picture is not like all others; it has a story of its own, I am sure, and you must tell me that story," she added, imperiously. Then changing her tone, she said in an appealing voice, " Darling, won't you tell me ? I do so want to know ! "

To this appeal Falcon gave in, despite his resolve to keep the dark legends of the house from his wife; perhaps he was not sorry to rid himself of the notion that he was deceiving her, concealing anything from her, however unimportant that thing, however, strong his reasons for concealing it might really be. Probably under any conditions he would have succumbed even to a less entreaty from his adored Lilith. Now he told her as shortly as he could what were supposed to be the facts of the story.

"That Cavalier, standing up with the drawn sword, is one of my ancestors," he said.

"He is not quite handsome enough for that," said Lilith, putting her hand on his arm, and resting it there, "but never mind."

"According to a legend, current for the time, the lady is his wife."

"And the other Cavalier ?" asked Lilith.

"The other Cavalier," Falcon replied, "was, as the legend goes, more to her than he should have been."

"Ah !" cried Lilith, with a sharp look of perplexity and pain.

"Whether this was so, whether there was any such cause of quarrel or sup- posed quarrel between the two men; whether there was a semblance of cause

which my ancestor exaggerated; whether
even such a scene as this ever took place—all
these are things unknown, and things which
would naturally find no place in our archives.
What is certain is that the legend, true,
false, or half true and half false, exists and
has made its mark, as you have no doubt
noticed, in Falcontree. However this may
be, do not let your little head be troubled by
such idle tales."

As he ended this speech Falcon gave
unconsciously something like a sigh and
turned to give a devoted look to Lilith, but
during the latter part of his recital, Lilith's
hand had slipped from his arm, and she
seemed to concentrate all her attention on the
picture.

"What can the painter have meant by
that look in her face?" she said, presently,
half to herself, "what is the meaning in her

eyes? It is not wholly grief, and it cannot surely be joy. I cannot explain it, but I must know some day."

Then turning round to Falcon, and banishing without any apparent effort the thoughtful mood into which she had fallen, she said—

" It is a clever picture and a dear old room, and a fine old organ, I am sure, and I was a little fool to dislike it, wasn't I? Come, sit down and play to me, darling. Or shall we wait until the room has been aired, and all gloomy fancies swept out of its corners? Come, then, and walk in the garden, and we will look down to the sea and wonder what makes it so restless, and we will play to-morrow, or next day. Come, dear."

She tripped out of the organ-room, followed by Falcon, as gaily as she had tripped out of all the others.

CHAPTER VI.

A FEW afternoons later Mrs. Thornton, the housekeeper, not without many anxious shakes of the head, and many liftings of the hands in sorrowful forebodings, announced that the organ-room was quite fresh, " as fresh at least," she said, " as such a room can ever be. Ah! my Lord! if you would but think over it before you stay in such a room. Ah! my Lady! if you could but persuade his Lordship."

But Falcon only frowned at her remonstrances, and Lilith laughed gaily and said—

" But, Mrs. Thornton, I don't believe the room is really different from any other room —not that I am at all sure of that really," she added, in an undertone to Falcon.

Mrs. Thornton went croaking away to

enjoy a debauch of evil prophecy with old Gillie, the gardener, and Lilith led the way with the fleeting run which was peculiar to her into the organ-room, whither Falcon followed her.

She was in a mirthful happy humour that day, and she caught him by the hand as they entered the room, saying—

"Now, dear, I shall look on this day as the birthday of your oratorio, which is going to be so good, so good! And when I hear it sung and played to listening masses of people, I shall be so proud of my Falcon! Not that I can be any prouder of him than I am now."

Then she led him up to the keyboard, and laying her tiny fingers on his shoulder, stood listening and attentive as he struck some powerful chords. So she remained until he had played four or five bars, and then she cried—

" What a magnificent tone ! is it not ? "

A glow of delight had come into Falcon's face as he recognised the power and beauty of the instrument which he played, and now he was too much absorbed to answer her except by a nod, from which she turned away with a little pout of petulance as if to leave him. But the subtle charm of the swelling chords was too strong for her, and held her seated at the window looking seawards as Falcon played on and on. He played, and she, with an unusual patience, remained to listen until warmer tints began to show themselves in the clouds first by streaks and patches, and then with a sudden glory of colour which changed to green, to orange, to purple, to all sorts of delicate shades for which art has no name, and of which Nature alone possesses the jealously-guarded secret. Then the white-crested waves rolling heavily in from the broad Atlantic caught the glow from above and swung it from one to the other until the whole bay, sea and sky, shone with the short-lived splendour. The music called out from the organ by the player's master hand seemed to Lilith's vivid fancy to join in the universal exultation; the harmonies rolled in greater fulness through the room; they seemed to have acquired suddenly a sense of freedom and delight in spreading themselves far and wide. It was as if a great river of melody had been dammed up years ago by the closing of the organ, and were now rushing out in a burst of joy at the opening of the flood-gates. As the music pealed on, and the deepening twilight lent it a yet more solemn effect, the associations of the place recurred to Lilith's mind as she listened. She imagined that with the melodies the spirits which had haunted the room were once more set free,.

and that their voices mingled with the deep tones swelling round the old oak panels. Now as Falcon struck a powerful major chord she seemed to hear a pæan of triumphant joy, of exultation in new found life and liberty : then as the major changed to the minor came mourning and grief, and passionate regret, mingled with pity for the rash hand which had broken the spell. And again in a passage of descending semitones she seemed to hear mocking laughter and fiend-like joy at renewed opportunities and hopes of working evil. So strongly did these twilight fancies affect Lilith's quick sensibility that she rose from her seat to banish them, and walked up to the picture. Falcon ceasing a few minutes later to play, and looking round, found her gazing at it with rapt attention.

"Studying the picture again, my pet ?" he said.

"I am trying to make out that expression

in the woman's eyes," she replied. "What is it like? I think it is the kind of look one might see in a tamed tiger that had suddenly tasted blood and resumed its old wildness. Ah!" She gave a little shudder and passed her hand before her eyes as if to shut out the impression produced upon her by the picture.

"My darling!" said Falcon, "I shall begin soon to think that there is really some evil fascination about that picture, and have it taken down."

"No, no, no!" she replied, "Falcon, on no account have it taken down; it interests me and gives me a continual puzzle for my little head. What can that look really mean? I must find out."

Lord Falcon returned to the organ the next day, and the next. Every time he touched its keys he seemed to draw out more and more its forgotten fulness; every time he left it he longed more to return to it; the joy of making it give out its volumes of sound became an absorbing interest, a passionate longing which he could not resist. Nor did he wish to resist it, for the tones of the organ seemed to stimulate his power of creating music to its utmost extent; sweeter and stronger harmonies came into his mind. His faculty of composing gained force, as it were, from the keys as he touched them. So remarkable indeed was the effect of the instrument that he said jestingly to Lilith one day—

" I really shall believe soon that there is some occult power in this room; it seems to inspire one with new ideas. What do you think, my kitten ? "

But Lilith only shook her head gravely.

He had been afraid at first of her resenting

his devotion to his oratorio, of her grudging
the time which he might otherwise have given
to her; but she encouraged him in his work,
and told him from time to time how great
would be her pleasure in his success. For
many days she would come into the room
while he was playing or composing, would
flit about with a lightness which could not
disturb him, encourage him with a swift
caress as she passed him, stop for a minute
before the picture and fix upon it one of her
penetrating glances, perhaps sit down and
look awhile at the sea-view, and then flit out
again as lightly as she had come in. Gradually,
however, as the days went on, she began to
exhibit occasional fits of petulance at Falcon's
constant devotion to his music, fits for which
she always begged forgiveness with the pretty
repentance of a spoilt child; but she came by
degrees less frequently into the organ-room,

and began to take drives by herself about the country. Lord Falcon noted the growth of this weariness on her part of his music, and felt that he could not be either surprised or indignant at it. It cannot be a source of unfailing interest to watch the slow progress of a work intelligible only to its creator, however deep may be one's attachment to that creator; least of all could such an employment be an enduring attraction to a person of Lilith's restless nature. Her husband, however, was unable or unwilling, or both, to break away from his work just at the time when he felt it expanding into beauty and life; and so he set about to devise some means of finding amusement and occupation for her until his task was completed. He abandoned at once the idea of asking a party into the house, for the attention which he would feel bound to pay them would disturb him in his studies. While he was musing over the difficulty, the thought of Arthur Vane came into his mind, and seemed to answer all the requirements of the case. Arthur was just intimate enough both with him and Lilith to make his presence in the house in no way a disturbing influence; he sympathised to a great extent with both of their tastes; Lilith had always seemed to like him; how then could he do better than ask Vane down for some little time? Accordingly he wrote an invitation to Vane, and went to inform Lilith of what he had done.

She received the intelligence strangely.

"What!" she cried, "you have asked Arthur Vane here without consulting me? Why did you do it?" she asked in a threatening tone, while she frowned at him.

"You used to like him," said Falcon, quietly.

"Have you forgotten," she said, "that Arthur Vane tried to come between you and me; tried to warn you against me? I have not forgotten it." Then she stood for a little while motionless with the same lost look in her eyes which had come into them on the day of Lord Falcon's proposal, a look as of one gazing far from the present into a dark future. Then recovering her gay manner, she turned to Falcon and said, "But I will forget it, dear. It was kind of you to ask him, and we will try to make it pleasant for him."

So saying she tripped away, leaving Falcon somewhat mystified by her behaviour. But he was accustomed to be mystified by her, accustomed to her waywardness, and thought very little more of it.

Arthur Vane at this time was beginning to be wearied of London: almost all his

K

friends had left it, and why he had not done so also was a puzzle to himself. Perhaps it was the interest which he took in Mr. von Waldheim's pictures which had detained him as much as anything else ; he liked to sit and watch the painter's practised hand at work, to listen to his shrewd, biting remarks, and turn over his portfolios of poetical sketches. Most of all he liked to lie lazily stretched on a couch in a cool corner of the room, so situated that the " Queen Mab " picture was before his eyes. As he gazed at it all kinds of fanciful stories came into his head, and these he always intended to work up into something worth writing, but that intention he never fulfilled. However, the studio was a never-failing attraction to him ; and now that he was deprived of this by Mr. von Waldheim's absence abroad, he felt that the time had come when he must go away somewhere. Oddly enough, invitations to two or three houses where he had always enjoyed himself before seemed to him now to augur nothing but dulness and insipidity, and he declined them one after another, in a vague hope or desire that he might receive one which should seem to him attractive and worthy of acceptation. Such an one he found, after having wearily turned over many other communications which lay on his table, in Lord Falcon's letter, which ran thus :

" DEAR ARTHUR,—Can I persuade you to come down and see us here for some time ? I warn you that you may find it dull. We are quite alone, and there is no excitement to be got out of the neighbourhood. But you will find plenty of subjects for sketches or verses, and by coming you will give us both a great pleasure.

" Ever yours,

" FALCON."

"The very thing!" said Arthur to himself. "I have long been thinking how I should like again to see Falcon and his wife. I wonder if she is changed since her marriage: I should think not. As to Falcon, I do not suppose anything would change him. I wonder if he's hard at work at his oratorio? Of course he is—there is an organ in the house. I wonder if she gets tired of it; it will be strange if she does not sometimes. However, the best way to satisfy all these wonders will be by going down."

It is more than probable that it was really a hope of receiving this particular invitation which had induced Vane to reject various others, although he did not acknowledge that fact to himself. At any rate, it was a peculiar circumstance that he should pass over several which promised all sorts of gaieties in which his heart was accustomed to delight, in favour of one which foretold nothing but quiet domestic life. However that might be, he wrote to accept it, and arrived a day later than his letter at Falcontree Hall.

He was received warmly by Falcon, and, to his surprise, somewhat shyly by Lilith. She hardly looked at him as he shook her hand, which did not return the friendly pressure of his. This unexpected reserve in her manner produced its effect upon him, and caused him to appear confused and ill at ease as he exchanged greetings with her; but she had entirely recovered her self-possession, when, a few minutes after Vane's arrival, they went in to luncheon.

" How has the organ turned out, Falcon ? " asked Arthur, presently.

" A perfect treasure," replied Falcon ; " it's tone is something wonderful, and the oratorio progresses well with its assistance. We will go into the organ-room after luncheon, and you shall tell me what you think of the instrument."

Vane was assenting to this, when Lilith interrupted him by saying—

"Not this afternoon, Falcon; it is too fine a day to be spent in-doors; I will show Mr. Vane the garden and grounds if he likes, and you shall play to us this evening after dinner."

"Ah, yes! that will be better," replied Falcon. "The fact is, that I get so absorbed in my music sometimes that I forget that it has not quite the same fascination for others which it has for me. Art is a tyrannical mistress, and her votaries are apt to serve her too well, perhaps. I shall have finished the first part of my oratorio before long, I hope, and then I will take a holiday. And now let us go and stroll in the garden."

The three started together, but Falcon left the others before long to go back to the organ-room. Vane, left alone with Lilith, felt a return of the embarrassment which he had felt at her reception, and after a short silence which seemed long to him, found nothing better to say than these somewhat fatuous words—

"I have not seen you since we met at Lady Vendale's ball."

"No," she replied, addressing him without any trace of the coldness which she had at first infused into her manner. "I remember that it was rather a nice ball. I had almost forgotten the existence of such things until you spoke of it. We are so remote from all gaieties here."

"You do not find it dull?" he asked, gently.

"Dull? No. There is much to see in the country round, and I like the quiet of our life, I think. Still," she said, with that confiding look which Vane remembered well, " I am not always good company for myself, and Falcon spends nearly all his days over his music. But now that you have come you will amuse me and talk to me, will you not? I wonder what we were talking of when we last met? "

"I remember, perfectly," said Vane, " we were interrupted in the middle of an interesting discussion on one of your favourite subjects—the supernatural. A purposeless kind of discussion at best, I am afraid."

"I do not like to think that," she said. " Are you convinced that there is nothing in it after all? "

" No, I am by no means convinced," he replied. " Sometimes I incline to think that

there is too much in it, which comes to the
same thing as nothing."

" It is the other end of the circle you
mean ? "

" Yes, or the same end—whichever you
prefer to call it."

" You know, I suppose, that we have got
a kind of haunted room here ? " said Lilith.

" I have often heard of the story," he
replied ; " I should like to see the room."

" We will see it in the evening," she said,
" not now, it is so pleasant out here in the
sun. Besides, Falcon is hard at work in the
room at his music. Listen ! Do you not
hear the sound of the organ ? Or, perhaps,
it is not Falcon, but the ghost who is playing
it. I have never heard the ghost, but sometimes I feel as if it were in the room. It is
a large dark room, and I cannot help fancying
at times that there is some evil, unseen

presence hovering in its recesses.   A foolish
fancy, is it not?" she asked, looking up at
him.

"A very natural one at all events in a
room of that kind," he replied.   "Falcon
would set it down to nervousness, and I
suppose he would be right.   One cannot
always resist such fancies, however.   But
here is no darkness, with the bright sun and
the flowers, and "—

"Yes," she said, interrupting him.   "Do
you like flowers?   Will you get me that
rose?   Thank you.   How sweet it is!   See!"
She held it up for him to smell as she spoke,
and then said, " Shall we go in ?"

In the evening they all repaired to the
organ-room, and after Vane had duly admired
the tones which Falcon drew from the instrument, Lilith, turning to her husband, asked
him to hold up a light to the picture in order

that Vane might inspect it. As the two men stood beneath it, she looked from it to them with an intense watchfulness.

" I should like very much to hear your version of that story," she said, presently to Arthur; "it is capable of many interpretations."

" I must study it more before I can venture to explain it," said Vane.

" Lilith has studied it most closely," said Falcon, " and I do not believe she has arrived at any satisfactory explanation yet."

" Not yet, not yet," she said, dreamily ; " but I will understand it some day. And now, Falcon, put out the lights, and let us see how ghastly the room looks in the moonlight."

Falcon, smiling at her fancy, extinguished the lights, and the room was illuminated only by the rays which came in through the deep window. The beams fell in a direct path through the panes on to the floor in front of the picture, leaving the rest of the room with its heavy furniture and panels in darkness which partly concealed the two men. Lilith, standing motionless in her white dress in the moonlight, recalled memories of Lady Macbeth walking in her sleep, of phantoms and spirits, of everything that was uncanny, while the faint moaning of the sea, heard far beneath the windows, added to the weird effect.

"Ah!" she said, presently, with a little shudder, "it is horrible, is it not? Let us go away."

As Lilith said good night to Vane at one end of the long drawing-room, while Falcon stood looking out into the night through the window at the other, she added—

"Do you know that I have borne some malice towards you for some time?"

" Towards me!   For what ? " he inquired.

" I heard of your visit to Falcon, when you tried to warn him against me," she replied, " and I was very angry with you."

Vane was taken aback at this speech, and his usual readiness of answer deserted him. He began a kind of confused apologetic explanation, which she cut short by saying—

" I have forgiven you now, and so it does not matter.   Only I felt impelled to tell you that I had rather hated you once. Now we are friends again, are we not ? "

" Friends always," he answered.

That night Vane had many dreams, in which the past and present were strangely mixed, and in which Lilith appeared under many guises.

CHAPTER VII.

LIFE at Falcontree Hall now went smoothly on for a week or two in a well-ordered groove. The three occupants of the place seemed to make a singularly harmonious party. Vane's intimacy with Lilith increased every day; he found it delightful to listen to her idle talk and laughter, and admire her graceful movements; nor was it less delightful to find her in a serious mood, when she would plunge recklessly into discussions of the most abstruse subjects, and break off with her pretty laugh when she found herself far out of her depth.

In all moods she was charming; most charming, perhaps because she had so many. Falcon, while these two went out sailing or riding together, worked with renewed vigour at his music, and looked with expectant pleasure for their praise or criticism of what he had done when they returned. One who had watched the tenor of their life for a few days from the outside would certainly have said, " Here is a wonderfully happy combination of things which make life most happy—devotion from an artist to his art; from a husband and wife to each other; from a friend to friends."

Yet Vane, in spite of the happiness which he found in this life, began, after a few weeks had elapsed, to make propositions for bringing his visit to a close, propositions which were invariably put aside by Falcon.

" What reason can you have for going, unless you are tired of us?" he would say. " You have no other engagements at present; and I think you know by this time that we are not likely to get tired of you. Bear with us a little longer yet; I cannot afford to lose your criticisms. Come and tell me what you think of my last chorus."

And Vane could allege no reason for hastening his departure, although, no doubt, there was a reason. But it was one which he dared not acknowledge to himself, for he felt that if he gave form and expression even in his own mind to his secret thought, he must at once and for ever give up a companionship which had grown very dear to him. Thus much he could not help feeling with regard to this thought which he had half consciously managed to hide away so carefully in the recesses of his mind that only now and again its ill-favoured head started up and forced itself for a moment upon his attention. It is dangerous work this hiding away of feelings which may be of serious import. Such a man as Falcon would have crushed a dangerous idea entirely and altogether, or would have taken such steps that its influence could no longer affect his actions : Vane, wanting the strength for this, fled himself before this feeling, instead of banishing it by the power of his will; and in his flight he was pursued surely if slowly, until one day he was fairly overtaken. He was talking with Lilith in the afternoon on the terrace, admiring the view far away and the flowers close at hand. She pointed to one of these, and said—

"Is not that a splendid rose ? He towers so high above the others, and looks down upon them with such supreme contempt."

" He is indeed fine. What is he called ? "

" Géant de Bataille. John of Battle, as my gardener always calls it; an appropriate name, is it not? Do you attach importance to names ?"

L

"In a way I do. I am always inclined to attribute certain qualities to names, and if I know the name of a person I have never seen, I draw a portrait of them for myself to fit the name. For instance, I always fancy Katie fair and flirting; Jack, jovial and amusing; Helen, dark and stately; Arthur, weak and irresolute, and so on."

"I do not think you are weak," she said, answering his unasked question. "Tell me what portrait you fitted to my name."

"I knew you and your name together," he replied.

"Ah, true!" she said. "And now you know us both better, do you not? It is a strange name, Lilith, is it not? Do you like it? Liking should grow with knowledge; will yours do so, I wonder?"

She looked at him inquiringly, with a smile on her lips and in her eyes, which tempted Vane to say suddenly and with energy—

"I could not possibly like you more than I do now."

The words had no sooner escaped him than he wished them unspoken, but Lilith appeared not to notice that they had any special significance, and only replied by her little purring laugh, with which she led the way into the house.

Vane went up to dress for dinner, and sat down in his room in a kind of despair. For now the thought that he had so carefully avoided seeing face to face had met him with a sudden shock in its full hideousness. Now he began to reproach himself bitterly for the persistence with which he had masked it beneath the smooth pleasantness of his daily life, even while he had heard many warning voices telling him of the passion smouldering in his breast, and would not listen to them. Even so had the Pompeians of old heard in vain the threatening groan bursting

from the bosom of the ground to tell them of
the fire raging within it; not the less had
they in the reckless daring born of idleness
and indulgence sung and danced in mad
gaiety, refusing to look further than the
crust of pleasant earth which lay between
their careless feet and the fury of flame
which presently broke forth and destroyed
them. And now the crust was broken
between him and his passion. No longer he
could blind himself to the fact that he loved
Lilith; no longer he could doubt that loving
her he must fly from her at once, ere he
stained his honour with a further confession
or a hint of his love. Now he saw with
terrible clearness of vision, as though some
screen that had kindly shaded his eyes from
a blaze of lurid light had been suddenly torn
away, not only that he loved her now but
that he had loved her ever since he had seen

her; that what he had taken for interest was growing admiration; what he had taken for friendship was passion. There was no doubt that he must leave Falcontree Hall at once; the longer he remained the greater would be his difficulty, and he had already stored up sufficient bitterness for his future. He must invent some excuse for his immediate departure; that would not be altogether easy, but some plan he must hit upon. He shrank from the thought of confiding in Falcon as a last and desperate resort; he had not the courage to expose his weakness, unless it became absolutely necessary; besides, such a confession would only make Falcon unhappy, and why should he inflict any part of his own unhappiness on his friend? He wondered if Lilith in any way suspected his secret. He could not think that she did; it was probable that she liked his companionship, would be

sorry to lose it, and imagined that he entertained no stronger feeling for her than that
of the friendship which she extended to him.
Otherwise she could not have received with
so much indifference the declaration which
he had made to her that afternoon in the
garden. From such harassing reflections as
these Vane was aroused by the necessity of
descending to dinner, where he bore himself
with a gaiety which, as is usual when one
feeling is assumed to disguise another, was
somewhat overstrained. His disquietude was
increased, moreover, by the consciousness
that Lilith, without appearing to do so, was
watching him with considerable attention,
surprised perhaps at his unusual flow of
spirits. After dinner they went into the
organ-room, where Vane found repose from
the strain upon his nerves in listening to the
music which soothed his troubled mind.

Falcon played the work of a great master, full of majestic peace, and Vane hearing was lifted for a few minutes out of the turmoil and misery of this careworn world into the rest and might of a higher one, a world of divine inspiration, of high aims fulfilled—of noble ends attained. This period of quiet did not last long however, for Lilith, coming over to where he sat, said—

" Will you come out on the terrace ? It is such a lovely moonlight."

Vane started, and all the trouble came back to his mind in an instant. He felt that far the best and wisest thing he could do would be to invent some excuse for refusal, but his nerves were unstrung by the struggle in his heart, and no excuse would rise to his lips. Besides, it was so hard to give up the last chance of seeing her, and listening to the music of her voice. Surely, he thought, no

harm could come of it; he had enough self-
control to conceal his feelings; they would
talk and laugh as if there were nothing to
trouble either of them, as they had many a
time talked and laughed before. He would
say good-night to her for the last time in an
unmoved voice, and the next morning his
dream would be over : he would leave Falcontree Hall and learn to bear his burden as best
he might. As he arrived rapidly at this conclusion, she said again—

"Are you coming?" and he rose silently
and followed her.

Arrived on the terrace, he found that he
had a little overrated his self-command, which
had been already tried severely ; he found it
impossible to begin at once the sort of lightly
touched conversation which he had suggested
to himself. So they stood a short space
silent in the moonlight, by the low wall

which separated the garden from the cliff sloping down to the sea.

In accordance with that strange inconsistency of human nature which calls trifles to the surface of men's minds when violent passions are tearing them in their depths, Vane found himself thinking how dangerous the place might be to any one ignorant of the depth beneath or careless in his movements. There was indeed, as has been said, a rugged path leading down the cliff, but any one who missed this would be in considerable danger. As Vane peered idly over the wall, Lilith broke the silence by saying, in a soft, sympathetic tone—

"I want you to tell me what it is that troubles you."

This was certainly the last question which he had expected to be asked; it took him completely by surprise, and redoubled his

difficulty. He stood astonished and speech-
less, and she went on—

"I have seen a change in you for some
days past, to-day especially. I know the
expressions of your face well, and I am sure
there is something on your mind ; do tell me
what it is. You have put so much confidence
in me, and we have grown to know each
other so well. We are great friends—real
friends, are we not ? and it is the business
of friends to help each other in their troubles.
Cannot I help you ? "

He made no answer save by bending his
head in mute sorrow, and she continued, this
time in slow and faltering accents—

"I have thought sometimes—as you will
not tell me your thoughts, I must tell you
mine—that I may be in some way the cause
of your sorrow ; I who, believe me," (she
laid her hand upon his as she said this)-

" would so willingly save you from any pain.
If it so chanced, it would be so much better
for me and for you that I should know the
truth."

She looked down as she spoke, and he,
moving a little way from her with a slow,
heavy step, ended his long silence, and broke
out in speech.

" Why do you torture me like this ? " he
cried. " Do you not see that your words
are true, horribly, desperately true? Do
you not see that every one of them stabs me
to the heart? Ah, no! how should you?
Why should I reproach you with my own
madness? But listen—for I must make my
confession once and for all. Do you hear the
wash and murmur of the waves on the coast
below? As the strength of those waves when
they are lashed to fury by the tearing gale,
as the endurance of that patient sea through

countless years, so are the strength and endurance of my love for you. I know now
that this began even from the first moment
that ever I saw you. It has gathered force
with time. I deceived myself as well as I
could; I kept my passion out of my own
sight, but it was there, just as the latent rage
is in those quiet waters. I was mad not to
see it, but I loved you too well to confess to
myself that I ought to leave you. Ah, well!
it would only have brought the end sooner.
I have had so much the more of happiness,
and now the end, ah, God! the end has
come."

So he spoke with a fierce volubility, leaning backwards against the wicket-gate,
clutching its rails with his hands, looking at
her as she stood motionless, while the tones
of the organ came fitfully out through the
open door. A cloud had driven across the

moon, and he could not see if her face was turned to him, or what expression it wore. He paused for a moment at the end of his wild words of love, and then dropping his voice, and taking a step towards her, he said—

"I have only two more things to say— Forgive me, and Good-bye!"

The clouds swept away, and the moon shone out in the fulness of her cold, cruel light as Lilith turned towards him. She was pale, and her lips wore a strange smile. He saw with amazement her hands stretched towards him, he felt his clasped in their warm grasp; a thrill of mad surprise and delight shook him as she lifted her face to his. Then, as a cloud obscured the moon once more, and the dying notes of the organ swelled sadly through the stillness, his lips met hers.

CHAPTER VIII.

FOR for some time after that evening Vane lived like a man in a mad dream of passion and wonderment : the world seemed to him . to have taken, now a new aspect of glory and joy, now one of relentless despair and gloom; to reflect from a million facets the beauty of the woman whom he loved, and the bewildering doubt whether she loved him or whether she was only playing with him a more deadly game than she had played with Frank Gordon. He was happy in lying at her feet, calling her his fairy queen, inventing new epithets for her wondrous fascination, while she looked down at him with the same strange smile which she had worn that night. He was happy in the long, loving talks which they held every night in the garden by the low wall, the scene of his first declaration to her: talks which were timed by the sound of the organ, for so soon as the last notes began to be heard, they would go in smiling to meet Falcon.

It was a dream of happiness, but a dream wherein was no calmness, no repose, and one which could hardly endure unbroken. Vane was not a man of evil nature: his better spirit had been first lulled to sleep by a slothful deadly charm, even as the Greek sailors were lulled by the Sirens' song, and had then been stifled for a time by the sudden grasp of an overpowering temptation. But when the first fierce waves of passion had spent their force and begun to subside and beat in regular rhythm, when his traitorous love became a part of his daily life, and the fascination of the danger attending it had lost its novelty, then by slow degrees the voice of the good that was in him rose up and made itself heard. For successful and consistent wrong-doing strength is necessary as much as for the doing of good, and Vane had not that strength.

He listened alternately to the voices of his good and evil angels, and could not compel himself to follow either one or the other with an unwavering purpose. He hung as it were helplessly between virtue and vice, stretching out his hands now to the former, now to the latter, and never stretching them far enough. The thought of the resolutions which he had made only to break them at the bidding of a woman's smile, of the unhallowed slavery to which he had bound his soul, of the kind trusting friendship which he had basely betrayed, would come before his mind at times in an aspect of stern truth. But Lilith's presence availed, for a long time at least, to dispel his moods of gloomy, barren remorse; to shake off from him the burden, which he sometimes felt to be very heavy, of his continual deception ; to soothe the anguish which every kind word from Falcon's lips inflicted on him.

Vane clung to Lilith's love as being both the joy and the support, if also the moving trouble of his life. The idea of her continued constancy to him was the one thing in which he found never-failing comfort. With the mad blindness of lovers, he forgot that her constancy had been already tried and found wanting ; that since she had proved disloyal to the man who had every claim upon her, she was not likely to prove loyal to him who had none.

It was when Vane was in one of his most unhappy moods, sitting on the terrace with his head supported on his hands looking

M

gloomily seawards, that Lilith came out and touched him lightly on the shoulder. He looked up, and the troubled expression which had been on his face vanished from it in an instant.

"I have got some news for you, Arthur," she said.

"Good or bad?" he asked. "But no news can be bad from your lips."

"I am not sure of that," she answered, with one of her strange smiles. "I do not think, however, that it can be very bad this time. It is only that Sir Harry and Lady Emmy are coming down here in a fortnight."

"To stay here?" asked Vane, anxiously.

"No, not to stay here; that might be awkward. It seems that the Normans have taken a large house some miles off, I do not know how many—I never know those things —but it's name is Colston Abbey. They have taken it for a few weeks, and are going to fill it and give a ball, and the Greys are to go there. Are you glad? Do you like Lady Emmy? Do you like her better than me?"

"I did like her much," replied Vane, hesitatingly; "whether I shall like her now is another question. I think I am rather afraid of her."

"Silly boy!" she said. "What should you be afraid of? What harm can she do to us?"

"I do not know that she can do any," replied Vane, "nor do I know why I should fear her, but I do."

"Nonsense," said Lilith, "you are weary and out of spirits, and full of fancies!"

Lilith, no doubt, was right in ascribing to Vane an unstrung, nervous, fanciful state of mind, for during the fortnight which was to elapse before the arrival of the Greys, a fancy of a most gloomy nature began gradually to take possession of his mind.

It was born, perhaps, of the mingling of certainty and uncertainty with which Lilith had filled his soul—a certainty that she was not true to Falcon, an uncertainty whether she could be true to him. She had seen his love for her before ever he had acknowledged it fully to himself; she had not only led him on to confess it, but she had so responded to the confession that he had been caught in the toils of an unworthy passion once and for ever. This was surely trouble, perplexity, and anxiety enough, but beyond this a new and bewildering phase of feeling came to stir and confound yet more the troubled waters of his soul, waters troubled assuredly by no angel. With his love for Lilith a vague sense of fear slowly mixed itself, intangible and subtle at first as unexpressed thoughts, resolving itself by degrees into the effect produced partly by her general bearing and conduct, partly by those stories of Frank Gordon and others, whose hearts her enemies had accused her of deliberately breaking, which now, for the first time, thrust themselves on Vane's mind as being possibly true. But it was not only that the remembrance of these stories would start up and vex his mind, not only that he seemed to detect in her almost unvarying lightness of heart a delight in the success of her systematic deceit as well as a delight in his love for her and her influence over him. To such ideas as these he thought he could assign their due weight or want of weight; could even dismiss them as empty imaginations; but there was another idea which he could not so dismiss, an idea caught from certain chance words and looks of hers, an impression of some unknown evil hidden in her mind; some dark spot of iniquity lying out of his sight, perhaps out of hers also. Of this idea, try as he might, he could not rid himself. He attempted in vain to ascribe it to the shadow over his own heart casting some of its blackness upon hers ; he attempted in vain to regard it as a diseased fancy born of wickedness, as foul weeds are of ill-kept soil ; its power was too strong for him. He became like a man conscious of being pursued by a phantom whose form he discovers vaguely or not at all. It came to him with the first dawn of daylight, and pursued him in his dreams; at times it would overpower him, and make him shrink away from Lilith even while she smiled upon him ; he found his only refuge from his horror in working hard at painting, at writing, at anything, so long as this dark fancy possessed his mind.

One day he had been fashioning some verses to chase the phantom away, when Lilith came into the room where he sat, holding a kitten in her arms. Standing behind him she took the paper from his hand and read over its contents, which ran thus—

> The waters raged but yesternight,
>   The wild wind raised a shrieking wail,
> The clouds drove by in swift affright
>   Before the fury of the gale.
>
> To-day the sea lies smooth as glass,
>   The storm-fiend's voice is heard no more;
> The waves in gentle cadence pass,
>   And melt upon the peaceful shore.
>
> The joyous ripple of the wave
>   Is like the sunny flowers that grow
> Upon the summit of the grave,
>   Yet cannot mask the death below.
>
> The glad sea smiles in the soft light,
>   A smile that can caress and kill,
> For yonder wave with crest so white
>   Bears a dead face that's whiter still.

"Clever boy!" she said. "But what is 'a smile that can caress and kill?'"

" If you do not know I can hardly explain it to you," he replied.

" I think I do know the kind of thing that you mean. It is the sort of feeling that I have sometimes for my kitten—haven't I, Kitty ?—or for anything that is soft and nice, and that I can caress. I would like to tighten my hold on its little neck, make it tighter and tighter yet until "—

As she spoke she suited action to word until the kitten cried out in pain and terror; but Lilith seemed not to hear it, she only wound her fingers closer round its throat, and Vane, looking at her, saw in her face so strange an expression of pleasure, that his fear for the kitten's life was merged in that indefinite fear of her which had before possessed him.

" Lilith," he said, gravely, " for heaven's sake, do not give way to such feelings."

" What feelings ? " she asked, with one of
her innocent smiles.

" I wish I knew. Surely you do not wish
to kill your favourite kitten ? "

" No. I only thought it felt so good to
squeeze. I did not want to hurt it, poor
little thing. Why should I ? "

" Your looks belied you strangely, then,"
said Vane with a sigh. " See : it crouches
away from you ; it loves you no longer."

" Loves me no longer? " she repeated,
angrily. " No ; it is you who love me no
longer. If you did you would never talk to
me like this : you would never have accused
me of cruelty : how can you do so ? " She
took up the kitten in her arms and fondled
and caressed it until, forgetting with its
short memory her past unkindness, it purred
with responsive gratitude. " The kitten
loves me as much as ever," she said, in-

dignantly; "it is you who have ceased to love me."

She ran into another room as she spoke, and Vane, having hesitated for a moment, followed her and, kneeling at her feet, pleaded with voice and eyes for forgiveness. While he yet knelt, and she half-petulantly granted him the forgiveness he begged for so earnestly, the door suddenly opened, and a servant announced—

"Sir Harry and Lady Emmeline Grey."

Vane felt himself shudder from head to foot; it seemed to him that his presentiment with regard to Lady Emmy was fulfilled; he felt powerless to extricate himself from the dilemma in which he was placed; but Lilith, who had drawn away from him as soon as she heard the motion of the door handle, said—

"Pray do not trouble yourself to look for

it any longer. It is of no importance."
Then she went on to Lady Emmy: "You
see I am no less careless than I used to be;
I have dropped my crayons, and Mr. Vane
was kindly looking for them. I am so glad
to see you," she said, greeting them both
warmly, while her eyes sparkled with secret
glee at her successful stratagem. "How long
do you intend to stay? A long time I hope.
Falcon will be so delighted to hear that you
have come. I will let him know at once."
She rang the bell intending to give directions
to a servant to inform Lord Falcon of the
Greys' arrival, when Vane, glad of an excuse
to get away for a moment and subdue the
agitation which this incident had caused him,
interposed, saying: "I will go and tell
Falcon. I shall find him more quickly, and
moreover I shall be glad to be the bearer of
such good tidings as those of your arrival."

"How do you like this old house?" said
Sir Harry, to Lilith, whom Lady Emmy had
eyed carefully, almost suspiciously, ever since
she had entered the room. She had seemed
also to shrink away from the other's
advances; her manner had been more like
Falcon's, less like her own than was her wont.
One would have said that she took no extraordinary pains to conceal that distaste for
Lilith which she had more than once
expressed to Sir Harry. Indeed, she liked
her no better now that she was Lady Falcon
than she had when she was Miss von Waldheim; on the contrary, the fact of seeing her
for the first time established as her brother's
wife seemed to recall with a new distinctness
all the unpleasant impressions which she had
formerly entertained with regard to her. Sir
Harry, aware of the unfavourable light in
which his wife regarded Lilith, had been

afraid lest Lilith should also become aware of
it, and out of the goodness of his heart had set
the ball of conversation rolling as well as he
could after Vane had quitted the room. But
his fears were groundless, for Lilith was, or
appeared to be, entirely unconscious of anything repellent in Lady Emmy's demeanour
towards her, and she assumed all the softness of manner which she well knew how to
assume, as she answered Sir Harry's question
about the house as much to Lady Emmy as
to him.

" It is most interesting. I have always a
liking for old houses ; and there is something
peculiarly romantic about this house, and
you know I was brought up to like romantic
things. The only danger is of being dull,
and we have avoided that most success-
fully."

" Ah ! " said Lady Emmy, in a voice

almost as soft as Lilith's, but directing at her unseen a quick glance of such apprehension and dislike as only her love for her brother could have called into her kind eyes. "It must be a great pleasure and a great resource for you to have Arthur staying here."

"Is it not?" said Lilith, with her happiest and most joyous expression. "Mr Arthur Vane is almost as much a *fanatico per la musica* as Falcon, and that, of course, is pleasant for Falcon and for me."

Perhaps no one could observe another person more keenly than Lady Emmy did Lilith as she waited for this answer; but beneath its bright cheerfulness she could detect no touch of embarrassment or pain.

"Vane is a very good fellow," said Sir Harry, "and a clever fellow too, and knows something about music, I believe. In fact, he knows a little of everything. I always think what a pity it is that he didn't take up one accomplishment and stick to it instead of devoting his talents to so many. But, then, if he had done that perhaps he wouldn't have been so popular."

Lilith looked at him with a pleasant smile, and said—

" I believe you are right. Success—real success—in any branch of art probably requires a sacrifice of popularity; do you not think so ? "

" Yes ! " replied Lady Emmy, with some vehemence; "but who would not sacrifice popularity to purchase greatness ? "

Lilith smiled to herself as she saw the repressed scorn and anger on Lady Emmy's face : she knew that she was thinking of her brother, and thinking that his wife did not appreciate his fine qualities. As she thought this her face caught something of her brother's expression; and Lilith seeing it, admired it more than she had ever done before.

So strangely mixed were the component parts of her character, that she never valued Falcon's noble qualities so much as at this moment, when she was using an apparent contempt of them to wound his sister. She had, indeed, begun to say, and with sincerity, that she held real greatness far above the superficial merit of popularity, when she was interrupted by the entrance of Lord Falcon, with Vane.

Lady Emmy embraced him with all the warmth which affection and anxiety can give, for she had been anxious about him ever since his marriage, and had come down to stay with the Normans more in order to satisfy herself of how things were going with her boy than with any other object. He responded to her greeting with the tenderness which he never displayed save to her and Lilith.

"I am so glad you have come, dear Emmy," he said; "but it is in a kind of hermitage that you find us. You will be pleased to hear that the oratorio goes on well; for which I owe many thanks to Arthur. He has been invaluable to me—to us—both as a critic and a friend. Has he not, Lilith?"

Lilith signified assent without a trace of discomposure, with exactly the blending of friendship and courtesy which the occasion seemed to require, as she looked towards Arthur; but he, feeling that the weight of his secret trouble had never been heavier than at this moment stood with downcast eyes, and the hand which he was resting on a chair close to Lady Emmy trembled in spite of himself. She saw it, and could not repress

N

a kind of half sigh, which she hoped escaped observation, as she replied to Falcon—

"You will break through your recluse habit, will you not, dear, to come to the ball at Colston Abbey? It is to be a costume ball, and, as there will be but few people, there will be plenty of room, which is not usually the case. You will come, will you not?" she said, forcing herself to address Lilith in a tone of kind invitation.

"Of course you will come," said Sir Harry; "one so seldom gets a chance of a pretty ball where there is room both to see and to dance, and the Normans are nice people. They take trouble to make things comfortable without bothering about what the world will say: I mean they think more of what the people who are there will say to it than what the people who are not will. I don't know if you see what I mean?" he

said, feeling as if he had got into a slight
confusion, and looking rather timidly round
for encouragement.

"I quite see," said Vane, who had to some
extent recovered his self-possession. "They
care more for the real effect upon their
guests than for the impressions of the outside world."

"Exactly so—exactly so," said Sir Harry,
with his contented laugh, and added, half to
himself, half to Lilith, "I said Arthur was a
clever fellow."

"Would you not like to hear the organ,
and some of Falcon's oratorio, Emmy?"
asked Lilith, with a slight hesitation before
she addressed her sister-in-law by name,
which until now she had avoided doing.

And perhaps with good reason, for Lady
Emmy's brows contracted slightly, and something like a faint reflection of her brother's

sternest expression came again into her face, as she replied, echoing the other's hesitation before she named her.

"Thank you, Lilith. I am afraid we must go back now: it is a long drive, and we shall be late if we stay longer. Harry, will you see if the carriage is ready?"

Lilith, with her prettiest air of insistence, accompanied Sir Harry on this errand, and Vane followed in her wake. Lady Emmy, left alone with her brother, laid both her hands on his arms, and looking up into his face with her sweet grey eyes, said—

"Well, my boy?"

"Yes, dear," he answered, divining her thought; "I am as happy as the day is long."

"God keep you so!" she said, and they parted.

When she and Sir Harry got into the

carriage, she leant back and crossed her hands over her eyes, as if to shut out some painful vision. Sir Harry, fancying that she had a headache, began to talk in a cheerful strain.

"Well, little Emmy," he said, "I hope you think better of Lilith—I was just going to call her Lilith von Waldheim—than you did. She seems to have made Falcon wonderfully happy. And what an excellent idea it was having Arthur to stay there. I believe Lilith is a very good, nice, little woman, but still you know she was always rather capricious and restless, and if she hadn't had somebody to amuse her she might have got bored with Falcon's music, though I believe she's thoroughly fond of him. And they seem to make such a pleasant party, to enter into each other's thoughts and wishes—a kind of happy family, don't you think so?

Nobody but Arthur could have answered the purpose so well."

Lady Emmy had removed her hands from her eyes, and sat pale, motionless, and miserable during this speech.   Now she rested her head on her husband's shoulder, and said to him—

"Harry, where are your eyes?   Or is it— which God grant!—that mine are blinded by some vile prejudice?   Yet I cannot think that it is so.   Would that I could!"

"Dear little Emmy! what do you mean?" cried Sir Harry, unused to see her so moved, and becoming alarmed.

"I mean this.   Did you hear Lilith say that she had dropped her crayons when we came in?   You heard that, but you did not see that there were none of the appliances for which crayons are needed in the room. My woman's eyes saw it.   Did you hear that she always spoke of Arthur as Mr. Arthur Vane? Did you see the gloom that overcast his face? Did you see him tremble when Falcon thanked him for his kindness? Did you see the triumphant glance that she shot at him as he followed her out of the room, at me as I went away? Oh, me! I dare not speak out the horrible suspicions that come into my mind, and yet I cannot banish them," she added as she spoke; and Sir Harry, now really frightened, petted and soothed her as best he could.

"My dear child," he said, "you must be ill; you have always had a kind of craze about that poor little woman; and now you are overtired and really hardly know what horrible things you are suggesting. Surely she may have dropped her crayons in a room where she was not using them; and what is there in her speaking of Arthur as Mr.

Arthur Vane?   It seems to me very proper
that she should; she is no near relation of
his, and you must remember that she does
not know us at all intimately yet.   As for
the look in her eyes, as I say, you have
always been foolish about them.   Do think,
dear, of what you have said."

   " I cannot help it," she answered; " I feel
so certain—I always did from the first, but
now doubly certain—that there is some evil
happening, or going to happen, to my boy,
and I cannot bear it.   I dread that woman,
and I fear my dread is only too well-founded.
God forbid that I should unjustly accuse her
of wickedness—that I have not done, nor
will I—but there is much harm that can be
done without what the world recognises as
wickedness.   She has it in her power to
destroy Falcon's happiness with a word or a
look, and I fear—oh, I fear so much!—that
she will abuse that power."

" Why should she ? " he replied. " I grant
you that in most cases there would be a
strong temptation to her to flirt with a young
man staying there alone with her and Falcon ;
and, for all I know, she might yield to it—
not that I think she would. And if Falcon
thought she was doing so, I dare say he'd be
miserable about it ; he's just the kind of man
who would. But remember Arthur, who is a
confirmed flirt, never flirted with her from
the first. You must recollect noticing that
yourself."

" My dear ! my dear ! " she said, " do you
not see that it is exactly there that the
danger lies ? "

" No ! Upon my soul I do not," said Sir
Harry.

He had spoken at greater length and to
more serious purpose than was his habit, and
now he seemed as much hurt as his good-
nature would allow him to be at the little

effect which his words had produced.   Lady
Emmy seeing this, and grateful to him for
his solicitude and attempts at comforting her,
smiled at him through her tears, agreed with
him that her fancies were, perhaps, the result
of fatigue or illness, and dried her eyes, trying to appear cheerful, as women after great
emotion can do, during the time of their
return to Colston Abbey.

CHAPTER IX.

LILITH and Vane met alone in the breakfast-room at Falcontree Hall next morning.

"Well, darling," she said as she came in, "where are all your fancies about Lady Emmy now? What harm has she done us?"

"None," he replied. "I do not believe she would willingly harm a living thing." Lilith pouted and tapped her foot impatiently on the ground, as was her wont when her humour was crossed. "But I feel a presentiment—call it a fancy, if you will"—continued Vane, "that through her and with her harm will come to us. There is a heaviness in the air, or in me: a sense of boding misfortune which I cannot shake off. Do not laugh at me."

"Laugh at you? No!" she said; "I am superstitious enough myself; but what can make you imagine such things about Lady Emmy? Find superstitious forebodings all over this house if you will—I believe there are plenty if we chose to hunt them out— but do not go out of it in such improbable directions to discover evil omens. Come, dear, and sit down to breakfast."

Lord Falcon presently entered, and the conversation turned upon the coming ball at Colston Abbey, to which it was decided that they should go. He said it would be a piece of gaiety for Lilith, as well as a relief for himself. He was happy in seeing his sister again, and a little harmless dissipation would save him from the chance of getting jaded with his musical work.

"What dresses shall we go in?" he said. "We had better all adopt the same period, and thus secure at least one harmonious group." Several suggestions were made and rejected, when Falcon said, "Let us go in the dress of Charles the Second's period. It is supposed to be hackneyed, and for that reason probably no one else will adopt it. It is always picturesque, and Arthur shall send sketches up to the costumier."

"Good heavens!" cried Vane. He was about to add, "Why, that is the costume of the picture in the organ-room," when something checked the words as they rose to his lips, and Lilith, casting a quick look at him, diverted the conversation immediately into some other channel. It was curious, that since the night on which she and Vane had met for the first time on the terrace, her interest in the picture had seemed to disappear; it had lost the extraordinary fascination which it had formerly possessed for her—or, rather, repulsion had taken the place of fascination; she avoided it as much as she used to seek it, and rarely spoke of it. When she went into the organ-room she scarcely looked at the picture, or if she did so, looked away again immediately. Vane, taking his cue from her in this, as he had done unfortunately in other things, avoided it also; and Falcon, pleased at first to find that she had ceased to trouble her head about it, had ended by never thinking of it himself and had probably forgotten, when he suggested the dress of Charles the Second's reign for the costume ball, that that period had any association with the picture. When they got up from breakfast, Lilith said in Vane's ear—

"I know what you are thinking of. Let us come and see once more if we can fathom the meaning of the woman's look in the picture." As he prepared to follow her, "No, do not come," she said, turning back; "do not look at it. Come out into the sunlight and forget it."

In accordance with Falcon's suggestion, dresses of the period which he had mentioned were ordered and sent down from London in time for the ball, which was to take place in a few days. In the interval Sir Harry appeared again at the Hall, but this time without his wife. He, worthy soul, had had it on his mind to discover, if he could, whether there were any grounds for his wife's suspicions as to a flirtation existing between Lilith and Vane—of more than a flirtation he entertained no idea—and had managed to ride over to the Hall alone, without letting Lady Emmy know of his intention. As he approached the house he saw Vane and Lilith sitting in a remote part of the terrace; and going to the door asked for Falcon, and was shown into the organ-room.

"How do you do, Harry? I am glad to see you," said Falcon. "I know you will not mind my attending to these keys while you talk. They have taken lately to ciphering—sounding on after my commands to them have ceased."

"Not at all; I like it," said Sir Harry; and then paused to collect his thoughts and wonder what he should say.

"It is fine to-day, is it not?" said the other presently, in an absent manner. "I have only just looked out on the terrace once."

"Yes," replied Sir Harry, "it is very fine; but it seems always to be fine here. I should say you have a very good time of it here altogether; and it was a good move opening the old house. I wonder nobody ever did it before."

" It has suited my purpose exactly," said Falcon.

"Just so—just so," said Sir Harry; and then, after another pause, in which he attempted, with no very brilliant success, to arrange some diplomatic query which should help him to a conclusion, continued, " You all seem to get on very well together ; " and having said it, felt horribly ashamed of himself.

" Get on well ? " repeated Falcon, looking up in some surprise. " Certainly we get on well. Why not? I have my music, and Arthur and Lilith were friends before my marriage."

" Of course—just so; friends before your marriage," said Sir Harry, feeling much confused and at the same time relieved. Then he hung aimlessly about for a few minutes, and finally said, " Well, I'll just go and look

for Lilith in the garden, and then I must go
back." As he went out of the room his eye
was caught by the picture, which he stopped
to look at. "That is a queer picture you
have there, Falcon," he said; "clever, but
with something quaint about it. What is
it?"

"It has a history of its own," replied
Falcon, "which I believe Lilith can tell you
better than I can. She was puzzled by it
when we first came down, but I think she has
solved whatever puzzled her by this time—or
given up trying to do so."

Sir Harry made his way to where Vane
and Lilith sat together on the terrace, and
presently began upon the subject of the
picture.

"Oh!" said Lilith, in answer to his
questions, "the peculiarity of that picture is
that no one can quite make it out. There is

a spell over it. I have been trying ever since I came here, and I have not quite succeeded yet. Will you try to break the spell? Spells are dangerous things to meddle with, are they not?" she said, turning to Vane.

"Indeed I believe they are," he replied, with an air of melancholy conviction which perhaps puzzled himself as much as it did Sir Harry, who soon afterwards took his leave and returned to inform Lady Emmy that he was certain her suspicions were unfounded, and that he had seen for himself that all was going well at the Hall. But she received his assurances with a doubtful shake of the head and a sigh.

In the time which elapsed between this visit of Sir Harry's and the ball at Colston Abbey, the heaviness and disquietude which Vane had described as hanging over himself, increased rather than diminished: and he had never felt the burden of his ill-spent days and the presciences of unknown evil press more hardly upon him than when coming down on the evening of the ball in costume, he found Lilith and Lord Falcon, also in costume, together in the organ-room, she standing under the picture, he dreamily playing soft melodies on the organ.

As Vane joined Lilith, Falcon started slightly, while his eyes moved from them up to the picture. They made a striking group, those three in the old oak-panelled room, and might well have been some of its former occupants recalled to life. Falcon, with his grave, handsome face, resembled one of the nobler men of that epoch, who looked sadly on at its frivolities and follies, wanting nothing but the power to check them. Vane's air and bearing were well suited to the hanging boots and white ruffles of a courteous

Cavalier, while Lilith was like a portrait of some court beauty which had stepped out of its frame in all the frippery and coquetry of the time. A sort of perfume of Charles the Second's court, with its gay laughter and its wicked revels, and its mesh of intrigue, clung to her as she moved about the room, followed by the admiring gaze of Falcon, while Vane sat moodily in a corner playing with the hilt of his sword and looking upon the ground. Presently a fancy seized Falcon, a fancy to him idle and harmless, to the others, or to Vane, at least, hideous, appalling in its mockery, charged with a fearful significance.

"Since we are assembled here in the costume of the picture," said Falcon, "let us make it a *tableau vivant!* Here is the very scene of the actual event, if there is, indeed, any truth in the picture or the story, to which I for one have never given much credence; and the costumes could hardly be more correct than they are. Come, Arthur! come, Lilith! You, I am sure, have studied the picture closely enough to play your part to perfection."

Every one of these words went like a stab to Vane's heart. It seemed to him the most diabolical mockery which could be devised that they two should stand up and assume in jest before Lord Falcon the parts which they were playing towards him in earnest; he felt as though it were an accumulation of evil upon evil, to go through such a ghastly pageant; and he shuddered silently in his corner as he heard the suggestion. But Lilith beckoned to him with her gayest smile to take his place.

As he assumed the required position, and sank to the ground to represent the dying man of the picture, a cry of surprise and horror escaped from him, which he thought he heard faintly echoed back from Falcon. The cause of this cry was the sight which he caught, as he fell, of Lilith's face, looking down upon him with so withering an expression of deadly passion, that the blood rushed back upon his heart, and he turned cold as he saw it. He read in her eyes—what, he knew not—but something, which he knew to be the fore-shadowing of the vague horror which he had dreaded for so long. It was some wild com-mingling of love and fury, of the wish to cherish and the longing to destroy, which he recognised as having seen hinted at in his dreams of her, if never in waking life.

Lilith, as this expression came into her face, and she saw the terror depicted in Vane's, laughed to herself her little purring laugh, for she knew that now she had fathomed the look in the picture's eyes.

Falcon, meanwhile, standing sword in hand,

unnoticed by them, in the attitude which he had assumed for the purpose of the *tableau*, surprised the glances which passed between them. And as on a dark night the vague forms of trees and houses can scarcely be distinguished in the thick blackness, until the lightning flashes and shows for an instant every outline clear and sharp in its deadly blaze, so by the light of that one glance, Falcon saw suddenly the whole lurid land-scape of their guilt, plain, in all its hideous-ness, before him. By its light he saw the dark view of the past illuminated with a blinding glare; he saw in a moment the truth of the warnings which he had received and neglected, the meaning of his sister's anxious looks and Sir Harry's visit; and in that moment he resolved to keep his terrible discovery from them at all costs. A thousand instances of careless words and deeds of

Vane's and Lilith's, trivial to him then, and colourless, showed black and guilt-stained now to his new power of vision, as they rushed swiftly through his mind. Every tone of her voice which he had loved, every pressure of the hand which he had inter-changed with Vane, seemed to rise up to his memory and proclaim their falsehood. The agony of rage, and shame, and revenge, the fate which had waited so long to gather its full force broke upon him in an instant; and as the blow struck him he reeled before it and shook the sword in his hand with a frantic grasp. Yet when the others turned and saw him he was standing firm and un-moved as before, and not a note in his voice quivered, as he said, with all his accustomed gravity of manner—

"An excellent performance, indeed. Your cry, Arthur, added greatly to the effect, although it was scarcely legitimate in a *tableau vivant*. Had we but moonlight here instead of candles, the representation would be perfect. And now it is time to start."

On the way to the ball neither Falcon nor Vane spoke much, but Lilith talked and laughed with her most fascinating joyousness. As they entered the ball-room, which was filled with a gay and motley crowd of mediæval knights and Watteau shepherdesses, Nights and Mornings, and brilliant uniforms, the same thought seemed to strike them all, as Lilith turned to Falcon with a questioning look, and Vane cast his eyes round the room with a scared expression.

"Yes," said Falcon, gravely, "it was at Mrs. Norman's ball that we first met, and at her ball we meet again now. Let us celebrate the happy occasion by dancing this waltz together."

As they swept round the room, many glances were directed at them, many remarks were made upon how well her light grace matched his graver courtesy; what a happy pair they seemed !

"I am so glad to see your brother again," said Miss Norman to Lady Emmy; "we were always great friends, as you know; and I am so pleased that his marriage has turned out so well: many people prophesied badly of it, but I always hoped it would prove happy. He looks a little pale and careworn, I am afraid, though; I suppose he has been working too hard at his music; he always did."

"He did," said Lady Emmy, in a tone, the sadness of which she could not entirely control; "but in that he always found his reward."

Miss Norman looked a little surprised,

and might have been betrayed into expressing her surprise but was claimed that moment by a partner. Vane meanwhile had disappeared in the crowd, from which he presently emerged to dance with Lilith. Ordinarily he was an excellent dancer, and his step went well with hers, but to-night the heaviness of his heart seemed to have communicated itself to his limbs; his feet refused to keep time to the music. At last he stumbled, and when Lilith reproached him with his awkwardness, he replied—

"I cannot help it; I cannot shake off the gloom which has come over me. All this bright music jars upon my ears; these brilliant lights are more bitter to me than the thickest darkness, and in every careless laugh I seem to hear a death-knell. Do not let me spoil your enjoyment, dear. I will plead a strained ankle, and go to play piquet with Sir Harry, who does not care for dancing."

"Poor boy!" she said, with a half-sympathetic, half-contemptuous accent, and was soon afterwards whirling round the room with another partner.

Lady Emmy was sitting out a dance with her brother in a remote corner of the conservatory, shadowed by tropical leaves. After a few trivial observations she laid her hand tenderly on his arm, and looking at him with her soft, steady gaze, said—

"Cecil, dear, I think you know how much I love you."

"I think I do," he replied, with a half sigh.

"Then let my love," she said, "the love which makes me think of you always with anxious care, as it did when you were a sweet little boy with such grave, thoughtful eyes, and with no one but me to pet and cherish you, and teach your hands to play the music that you longed for—let that love be my excuse if I offend you in anything that I say now."

Falcon's brows contracted slightly, and his mouth grew set, but he answered—

"Dear, you cannot offend me."

"I do not know how to speak what is in my mind," she said, clasping his arm a little tighter; "it is very difficult, the more because it is so long since I have seen you and talked to you like this.   But somehow it must be said." She buried her face an instant in her hands, and then lifting it, she said, "I cannot help feeling uneasy about Lilith, and I cannot rest till I have told you so. I have said it—it has cost me much pain and fear to say.   Are you angry ? Do not look away from me—do not take away your arm."

He moved back his arm, which he had taken
away at the mention of Lilith's name, and
took Lady Emmy's hand in his, but he did
not turn his face to her as he answered,
" I cannot be angry with you ; least of all
when I know well that your words spring
from your love for me ; but give me more
proof of that love, I beg you, by never saying such words again. I know well what
you—I will not say suspect—but fear. Let
me assure you, once and for all, that any
fear which you may entertain of my wife
doing anything even in the merest thought-
lessness which could make me uneasy will
be entirely without cause. I know her
thoroughly." As he said this he clasped his
sister's hand with a sudden pressure. " I
have never blamed you," he went on, "for
the slight prejudice which I knew you always
entertained against her ; it was but natural.

And I repeat, so far from being angry, I am grateful, as ever, for your thoughtfulness and your love." He turned his face to her as he concluded, and it appeared to her as if all the lines on it had suddenly deepened, but this might have been caused by the shadows cast from the large tropical leaves under which they sat. He bent and kissed her once tenderly, and then took her back to the ball-room. Perhaps even the moment at which the knowledge of his wife's falsehood had flashed upon him did not cause more pain to every fibre of Falcon's nature than did the telling of this deliberate untruth to his sister. The one had been a sharp, sudden, over-mastering anguish; the other was an effort for which he had prepared himself, and which he had determined to carry through. He was one who suffered in silence and alone.

CHAPTER X.

WHEN the three returned to Falcontree Hall the moon was shining calm and bright on the sea, chequering the avenue with the shadows of leaves, casting dark shades on the terrace in front of the house. A common impulse seemed to guide their steps to the organ-room.

"You seem out of spirits, Arthur," said Falcon, as they sat down. "I only saw you dance once, and that was with Lilith."

"Yes," answered Vane, absently; "she was kind enough to promise me an early dance."

"And she kept her promise?" asked Falcon, with a marked emphasis.

"I am not in the habit of breaking my promises," said Lilith, petulantly.

P

"Are you not?" said Falcon. "Do you only break hearts, then?"

There was something strange in his manner, but Lilith appeared not to notice it, and replied carelessly—

"I do not think I can have broken any to-night; they were all too fat and stupid."

Falcon looked at her with a weary smile, and sat down to the organ.

"Have you got the keys into order yet, Falcon? You will have finished the first part of your oratorio soon, will you not?" said Lilith.

"In a day or two, no doubt," he replied. "I shall be both glad and sorry when I have got through it. Sorry because it must be the signal for our breaking up; and we have been such a happy, harmonious party, have we not?" he said, without varying the usual calm inflection of his voice, but looking from one to the other with an undisguised scorn, which was not perceived by Vane, whose eyes were cast upon the ground, and was unnoticed by Lilith. " But we may break up sooner even than in a day or two," added Falcon, in a tone so different from his ordinary one as to be almost brutal.

Lilith shrugged her shoulders, and as Falcon began to play, crossed over to Vane, who had rather kept apart from her since their return, and said, in her caressing voice—

" Come out and see the moonlight."

He muttered—

" Not to-night," without looking up.

Then bending down, she said in his ear—

" Come, darling," and he rose with slow, reluctant steps, and followed her. They passed from the organ-room to the entrance hall, and thence on to the terrace by the open door, through which the broad beams of moonlight coming in, seemed to meet the issuing flood of music and mingle with it.

"Why did you bring me out to-night, Lilith?" cried Vane, as they neared the terrace wall.

"Why Arthur! what a question! Because I love to have you here all to myself for a little. I have scarcely seen you all day. Look how bright the moon shines on us as we stand! I love the moonlight."

"Bright!" said he; "yes, with an unhallowed light. There is nothing good—nothing human in it. She hangs up there in the sky, the spectre of a dead world, and her light is the light of corruption which shines from death. Ah, Lilith! the moonlight has been a bad light for us, I fear!"

"Bad!" she cried, moving away from him. "You call it bad and say it is not human when I tell you that I love it. Bad!

you call it bad when it has shone for us on so many happy nights, when it was by this light that I first heard you tell your love for me! Arthur! have you forgotten so soon? Have you wearied of me so soon?"

"Wearied of you?" he cried; "my fairy —my queen! How can you speak so? Do you not know by this time that I can never weary of you so long as body and soul cling together? that your presence is as the breath of my life?"

He drew her close to him within his grasp.

"Hark! What is it that Falcon is playing?" he said presently, bending his head away from her towards the door. "Good God! it is Bach's *Judas* music!"

He shuddered and dropped his head upon his breast as he spoke; but she, clinging closer yet to him, looked up in his eyes as she said—

"Why do you look like that, my darling?

Do not think of horrible things. Think only of me, who love you, who am here close to you."

They stood a few moments with arms interlocked in the cold moonlight, until she too, shuddering, cried—

" Ah ! what is that ? " as a horrible discord broke like angry thunder from the keys, and bore its harshness through the open door.

Then, turning, they saw Falcon standing behind them with his sword drawn in his hand, tall and stately, like an avenging spirit, while still the organ pealed on in jarring dissonance.

" Ah ! " cried Falcon, with a harsh laugh ; " the picture is complete at last ! " and turned sternly on Vane.

Vane laid his hand on his sword, and had just drawn it from the scabbard when his eye fell upon Lilith, who had broken away

from him at the first sound of her husband's
voice. She stood with her hands stretched
towards him. The attitude, the place, the
light, were the same as they had been on the
evening when first he told his love to her,
but on her face now was a look which un-
nerved his arm and made him drop his sword
to his side. It was the look of which he had
so many times seen the subtle indications,
the same look which she had worn when they
rehearsed the scene of the picture, but in-
tensified, now that the picture was indeed
complete, to a tenfold horror of tigerish joy
and ruthless craving for destruction.

Many a time Vane had longed to tear off
his false mask of friendship and meet Falcon
face to face and sword to sword, but now he
quailed before the look in Lilith's eyes, and
retreated cowering as Falcon advanced upon
him, until, still gazing at her in horrible

fascination, he struck his foot against the base of the low wall which separated the terrace from the cliff, and, stumbling backwards across it, hung helpless over the cliff. Falcon stretched out a hand to save him; but clutching wildly at the coping of the wall, he missed it and went headlong down; while the organ gave one last exhausted wail of unearthly discord, as though evil spirits had seized upon the pipes and keys. At the same moment Lilith with a moan of terror fell motionless on the ground.

An instant Falcon looked at her, and then going quickly back to the house, rung up the servants.

"Send Lady Falcon's people to her at once," he said; "she has fainted on the terrace. Mr. Vane has had a terrible accident. That wall! I should have had it heightened long ago. And bring lanterns quickly down the cliff path with me."

The servants assembled in hurried confusion; Mrs. Thornton, the housekeeper, finding time to say in the ear of old Gillie, the gardener, as they went off, he to bear a light down the cliff, she to attend to Lilith,

"What have we said many a time, Mr. Gillie, that harm would come of opening a house marked out with a curse? And so, even as we said it, it has come true now. Poor Mr. Vane! so young and so pleasant in in his ways. I do hope as you may find him alive."

The party of servants, headed by Falcon, descended the rugged path in the cliff carefully and cautiously, holding their lanterns up and peering here and there at every turn to see if they could find what they sought; making a thin line of sharp yellow light among the dark foliage, while the moon cast a grey, indistinct haze around them. Right down to the foot of the cliff they threaded their slow, anxious way, coming every now and then upon traces left in the bushes by Vane's feet and hands as he had clutched and torn at the branches in his headlong descent. Close above the slope of the cliff to the beach, resting on a ledge of barren rock, they found his body bruised, mangled, and lifeless.

Falcon walked silently back with them as they bore the corpse to the hall, and laid it in one of the large rooms. Then he went to look for Lilith, whom he found in her own room, crouching in a corner, pale and trembling.

As he entered, she tottered towards him with a faltering heavy step, most unlike her usual light run, and falling at his feet she caught his knees with her hands, and seeing the stern look on his face, cried, in broken accents—

"Falcon! Cecil! pity me! oh, pity me!"

"Pity!" he repeated, looking down at her

with such intolerable scorn that she dropped her head and hands as if he had struck her. "Pity! What should you know of pity? What pity had you for me when you deceived me with your soft looks and wiles? What thought of pity had you when you took my heart in your hands, the heart I gave you so trustingly, and crushed it in your weak, deadly grasp? What did you know of pity when you took his life into your hold and murdered him?"

She gave a low wail of agony and crouched yet lower to the ground.

"He will never look for your smile, never listen for your voice again. He has paid for your crime and his with his life. And shall no payment be exacted from you?"

She trembled and shrank away from him.

"No, do not fear; I am not going to kill you; for such inhuman devilry as yours what human punishment can avail? I have

decided on your future so far as I am concerned with it. To-morrow you will go back to
your father. When you are once in his
keeping, you and I shall be as strangers on
the earth. Of the reasons for this the world
will know nothing. You have blasted my
life, but you shall not tarnish my name. You
hear my voice for the last time now, and with
my last words I bid you go and learn what
pity is."

She lifted her head, and made a gesture as
though to catch at his hand, but he turned
from her in scorn and left her.

Falcon spent the remainder of the morning
in arranging affairs according to the plan
which he had found determination to conceive
between Vane's fall and the recovery of his
body. He wrote to Lady Emmy, telling her
that Vane had fallen while they were all three
walking on the terrace, blaming himself for
the terrible fate which had overtaken him, in

that he had not looked earlier to the dangerous lowness of the wall; announcing that Lilith was so upset by the accident, of which she had been an eye-witness, that he should send her back at once to London, where her father now was, out of sight of the painful associations of Falcontree Hall. He wrote to Mr. von Waldheim, briefly detailing the facts which had occurred without any comment. This letter cost him much to write. Mr. von Waldheim received it a day before Lilith arrived, and part of that day he spent in a mad outburst of fury and despair, which left him only sense enough to lock his door and struggle with himself alone until the storm of his passion was exhausted and had subsided from mere want of endurance. He knew Lord Falcon so well, by the sympathy which exists between strong natures, that he could not doubt the truth of what was told to him. Therefore he accepted it as a fact at once;

but the anguish in which he writhed helpless, as Prometheus may have writhed, under the knowledge of his daughter's disgrace, was not the less for that.

When this first access of rage and horror was subdued, he fell into a kind of lethargy, which was upon him when Lilith arrived and fell miserably at his feet, having nowhere else to fling herself, so that he put his hand upon her head with a few broken words of sorrow, as though she had been the little child whom he remembered coming to him penitent from some naughty prank. This lethargy grew upon him day by day, while she stayed with him, as she did to the end of his life. By slow degrees he grew feebler and feebler in his powers of mind and body, until at last he used to sit a broken wreck, with the mouth that had once been so firm weak and drooping—with the eyes that had been full of fire dim and wandering, dabbling a dry brush on an empty canvass, and appealing to imagined crowds of admirers whether his work was not the best that he had ever done. "Beautiful is it not?" he would say. "A painter knows his own skill, and this, I assure you, is beautiful. Full of grace and full of power, and all taken from my daughter; is it not, Lilith? Will not Lord Falcon like it? Vane used to say it was such a good portrait." And Lilith gave assent to all his questions, fulfilling thus that punishment which Falcon had said no human power could inflict upon her.

On the same day during which she arrived at her father's house Vane's funeral took place. Falcon, pale and with dark circles beneath his eyes, but upright and firm in his gait as before, attended it as chief mourner. The villagers followed him, all mourning for the death of the young man whom they had liked, but yet with a latent unacknowledged satisfaction in their hearts at the fulfilment of the evil prophecies which they had made as to the re-opening of the hall. After that, Falcon, writing to his sister that he was ordered abroad for the sake of his health, which he had unconsciously injured by over-work at music, and that, much to his regret, he was obliged to leave his wife behind to take care of her father, for the present left England. Lady Emmy is still anxiously awaiting the time when she shall embrace her boy again; if that time ever comes, the embrace will not be given at Falcontree Hall, which is shut up once more with a seal on the door of the organ-room. Meanwhile Sir Harry is loud in praise of Lilith's devotion to her failing father.

AN EPISODE IN THE LIFE OF MR. LATIMER.

Q

AN EPISODE IN THE LIFE OF MR. LATIMER.

I.

Theophile Gautier, in "La Pipe d'Opium," relates the strange opium-born dream in which he found himself again smoking that intoxicating drug with M. Alphonse Karr, and suddenly observed to his host that he had had the ceiling repainted, to which M. Karr replied—

"Le plafond s'ennuyait apparemment d'être noir, il s'est mis en bleu ; après les femmes, je ne connais rien de plus capricieux que les plafonds ; c'est une fantaisie de plafond, voilà tout, rien n'est plus ordinaire."

This explanation has always appeared to me to be exceedingly pleasing and capable of wide application to all sorts of events which without its existence would clamour vainly for expounding. If there ever had been—as there was not—any danger of my forgetting it, frequent companionship with Charlie Morton would have served to keep me reminded of it. Neither woman nor ceiling could be more full of caprices than Morton, and the unexpected way in which he took up for a time pursuits between which and himself one could discern no kind of connection made the " fantaisie de plafond " explanation peculiarly applicable to him.

Among other things, constant as he was to his friends, so long as he did not see any of them for too long at a time, he loved to be constantly surrounded in his daily life by new faces, and therefore frequently changed his servants—except his cook, whom he never saw, and a kind of body-servant and steward in one, who was an attached and admirable servant, and who, at certain intervals, either sojourned in the country for a time, or managed, if his master were in special need of his services, to make considerable changes in his facial appearance, and even in his voice. To this man, Thompson, was entrusted the duty of engaging and dismissing the other servants, and knowing well his master's fondness for absolute novelty, he sometimes went rather out of his way to engage people who had some peculiarity of appearance.

I went once to a bachelor dinner with Morton, just after the end of a certain agitation concerning modern sorcery, in which he had been taking a lively interest, urging whatever influence he could against certain people whom he denounced with an anger and a disbelief in the possibility of spirits, ghosts, and *diablerie* of all kinds, of which the violence was for a time, as with most of his quickly taken up and dropped fancies, amusing.

In Morton's house, on the evening of which I speak, there appeared a new butler, in which there was nothing strange; and this new butler was a very odd-looking fellow, and in this too there was nothing strange. But he was perhaps the oddest of the odd lot that I had seen there. He had a yellow parchment-like face, the skin of which seemed to have been tightened like a drum-head, none of his features fitted each other, and his curiously piercing black eyes, the seeming youth of which was in odd contrast to the aged look of the rest of the face, had in them a strange expression which I could not fathom; indeed the man's aspect had an odd fascination for me, and I was both startled and ashamed when I was roused from a reverie in which I must have been half-unconsciously staring hard at him, by his asking me what name he should announce.

It may be purely fanciful to note that when I gave him my name—which had lately appeared at the bottom of an article concerning superstitions ancient and modern—I thought I detected a curious lighting up of the young eyes in the old tight-drawn face, and that his carefully subdued and respectful tone of voice seemed to me to convey a curiously grating—I cannot say note, but impression. It reminded me, I could not tell why, for there was no defined likeness, of the terrible Coppelius as described by Hoffmann in "Der Sandmann."

Knowing Morton as I did, I was but moderately surprised at finding from the dinner conversation that his late crusade against superstitions concerning "witches and other night fears" had led him to look more into the subject, and as a consequence to entirely change his point of view.

The question was one which had always amused, and in the hands of such writers as Hoffmann and others, delighted me. We talked of Hoffmann's stories, of Gautier's "Deux Acteurs pour un Rôle," of Cazotte's weird "Diable Amoureux," and of the extraordinary gift of prophecy assigned to Cazotte himself in a well-known story. We went on to discuss Cazotte's interview with the mysteriously cloaked *Illuminatus,* who puzzled him by giving mysterious signs, of the stranger's surprise at finding that Cazotte "did not know what the " (here the new butler drowned a word in a clatter of plates, awkwardly dropped) "to make of them," and of Cazotte's being then as a matter of necessity admitted as a neophyte into an Order of which he was supposed from his book to be already a member in the highest grade.

Presently, when dessert was on the table, Morton, who had all this time been talking with enthusiasm and liveliness, cried to me—

"Darsie, did you ever come across a queer old romance which was written by James Hogg, and which is called 'The Confessions of a Sinner?'"

As it happened I knew this very remarkable and now half-forgotten book intimately, and we proceeded to discuss it at some length. We agreed that it was one of the best imagined and and best executed tales of *diablerie* ever written; that the Defoe-like and ingeniously dovetailed details of the dark narrative carried conviction with them as one read; and that it was very easy to rise from reading them, agreeing with Mr. Toobad, in "Nightmare Abbey," that "the Devil had come among us, having great wrath." The book is one which I have always admired, and I should have thoroughly enjoyed talking over it but for the constant interruptions of the new butler, who was for ever finding some more or less frivolous pretext for entering the room and hanging about the table. Oddly enough, Morton, who was generally excessively fussy about interruptions of this kind, appeared to be quite unconscious of the bad training exhibited by his new butler.

In the smoking-room after dinner the conversation took a different turn, and the only reference to what we had been talking about was found in Morton's announcement that he meant to call a new racer of his " My Illustrious Friend," the title given to the tempter by the tempted man in " The Confessions of a Sinner." The new butler, somewhat, I confess, to my relief, did not appear in the smoking-room.

As I was going away, Thompson came

forward to me in the hall, offering me a light for my cigar, and I was just going to make some half-chaffing inquiry of him as to the queer fish he had engaged as butler, when he suddenly disappeared, in obedience, as I supposed, to some call from his master, and I found myself face to face with the new butler, who presented to me, not a lighted match, but a large volume bound in vellum, fitted with a lock, and bearing a strange Eastern-looking inscription in red characters. With the same rather uncanny modulation of voice that I had observed before, he asked if I would favour Mr. Morton by writing my name in it—it was an idea that he had lately started to keep an autograph record of his guests. The thing in itself surprised me little or not at all, for Morton was quite capable of taking up that or any other whim, but it did seem to me strange that Morton himself should have said not a word about this new fancy. This, however, was but a momentary impression, and carelessly taking up the gnarled goose-quill which was put into my hand charged with red ink, I was about to sign my name, when the very odd appearance of the new butler again caught my attention and delayed the movement of my fingers. Probably he misinterpreted my hesitation, for turning over the pages, he said—

" I can assure you, sir, we have some very distinguished names in this book."

As he spoke a curious change came over him or over me—a change which I was, on after-reflection, more than willing to attribute to my having followed up some excellent Bordeaux by some equally excellent Madeira. His youthful eyes seemed to flash with a baleful fire, his old parchment-like skin to be suddenly covered with innumerable wrinkles, or innumerable characters of woe and horror. Fire seemed to scintillate from the claw-like fingers with which he held the pen, and to follow his footsteps as he moved towards me, while in his whole aspect there was an air of hideous, but withal majestic, triumph. In fine, I felt quite suddenly that, whether having great wrath or not, the Devil had come amongst us. At the same time I felt a curious longing to sign my name, and in the signing, as I felt in spite of the longing, to incur consequences which might at least be serious. Suddenly a happy instinct came to my rescue. Holding the pen, with fingers impelled against my will, close to the paper, and looking at the new butler, who now seemed again to be just such an odd fish as I had thought him at first and nothing more, I said—

" I will sign on one condition."

Again I thought I saw a fiendish gleam in his eyes as he answered—

" Any condition you like to name—any conditions—whatever you please."

Then, tapping him on the shoulder, I said kindly but firmly—

" Reform, dear boy, reform."

For a moment he gasped, his parchment-skin assumed a dull red hue, as of fire flowing through it, and I knew not what next to expect, when Thompson approached me again with a light, the new butler resumed his normal appearance, and I wondered how my Madeira-heated fancy could have conjured up the Devil out of a queer, shambling, honest fellow, whose only really remarkable oddity was the contrast between his eyes and his skin. As I was going out, Thompson called to me—

"Beg pardon, Mr. Latimer, your shoe-strings are hanging so long that you may trip over them."

The new butler, with respectful eagerness, pressed forward to fasten them tighter, but the odd waking dream I had had about him availed to make me wave him off with thanks.

Once in the air, and with a good cigar of Morton's in my mouth, I could not but be amused at the queer result of our *diablerie* talk. Indeed, when I had walked half-a-mile or more, I found myself laughing out loud, and at the same moment stumbled over something and fell, catching myself such a crack over the sconce that for a few seconds I was half unconscious. When I came to myself, I found four or five persons round me, one of whom was descanting upon the monstrosity of leaving open the coal cellar trap over which he said I had fallen. Unluckily I knew better. I had seen as I fell, and I saw now, that the real cause of my tumble was the exceeding length of my shoe-strings, which had caught in Morton's door as I went away, which had lasted me for the half-mile or more I had walked, and which had then pulled me up without warning. Indeed, so well did I know this, that my first speech was an entreaty to have the strings cut which held me prisoner.

"Poor gentleman," said one of the little crowd, " he ain't quite come to himself—he's wandering, like ; " but at the same moment a policeman, with piercing black eyes, and a yellow skin, under cover of bending down to look after me, cut the strings with his truncheon as if it had been a knife, and helped me to my feet.

He then observed with admirable hypocrisy

that I ought to take proceedings against the owner of the coal-cellar flap, and asked me for my name and address. In the agitation of the moment I was about to give him these, when he said, with a voice which I recognised in spite of his attempt to disguise it, that it was well to have these things in writing, and produced a book which was the facsimile in little of the one produced by Mr. Morton's butler. The small crowd, with characteristic love of meddling, urged me to take this excellent advice, when I remembered the presence of mind displayed by the old gentleman who met an escaped lion in Piccadilly. His case was better than mine, for a menagerie lion may very likely be as frightened at his new freedom as are the people that he meets, whereas the lion whom I had met was, I knew on good authority, constantly seeking whom he might devour, and seemed specially anxious to devour me. However, I followed the old gentleman's example, and hailing a hansom which came up attracted by the disturbance, I leapt swiftly into it, and drove away amid the hoots of the lately sympathising but now indignant crowd.

These events were, it may be admitted, exciting enough, but I had not yet done, as I felt sure when I got up the next morning, with Mr. Morton's butler. The first thing I did was to make some excuse for calling at Morton's house, and getting a word with Thompson. I tried to refer in a casual and airy manner to the new butler, but I felt quite sure that Thompson, who replied in the same tone, knew as well as I did, and was equally unwilling to confess, that there was something more than common about his latest acquisition in the servant line. I gave some brief account of my accident, and said with as little effort as I could—

"By-the-bye—but I suppose it must have been fancy—I thought I caught sight of the fellow in the crowd round me."

"He did not leave the house, sir," said Thompson, gravely.

"Precisely," I rejoined, and the utterance of that very commonplace word made me feel meaner than I have often done in my life.

A few nights after this I was going to hear what the extreme left of the Wagnerite section call "the disgusting olla-podrida of Meyerbeer," in *Robert le Diable*, and I may here observe that, apart from the merits or demerits of Meyerbeer, it is a good joke to speak of an olla-podrida as disgusting, though to be sure it might be made so by German cookery or uncookery, which can,

when it likes, be very " curious and disgusting." I went with an old friend of
mine, an operatic critic, in a small box on the
third tier.

It was my friend's habit to jot down notes
of the performance as it went on, in his
libretto, and just before the overture began
he discovered that he had forgotten his
pencil. I rummaged vainly in my pockets,
and he was about to apply to a box-keeper,
when a man sitting in an end stall on the
other side of the house got up, and with a
polite bow stretched his arm, his hand holding
a pencil, right across the theatre up to our
box. This surprising incident took place in
a house nearly full of people. Not one of
them took the slightest notice of it. All my
friend said was—

" So you have found a pencil at last?"

Of course, I knew who it was who had done

this, and waited with a kind of dumb resig-
nation for what was to come next. Between
the acts the man in the end stall levelled his
opera-glass at us—I could feel the piercing of
his eyes through it, or rather, the eyes seemed
to have taken the place of the lenses—and
moved from his place. I tried to get away,
but my friend kept me in talk, and in a
minute came the tap which I expected at the
door. There limped into the box a spare,
loosely-built, heavily-bearded man, with a
parchment skin and flashing eyes.

"Mandeville!" exclaimed my friend with
effusion; and I must say the name struck me
as curiously appropriate. He then explained
to me that I had often heard him talk of his
old friend the well-known traveller, Captain
Mandeville, which was not true, and introduced us to each other. The captain be-
haved with exemplary politeness, and pre-

sently fell into more or less confidential talk with my friend, casting now and again a curious glance at me.

"Darsie," said my friend, just before the curtain rose again, "Mandeville has in his possession part of an early draft of the score for *Robert le Diable.*"

"To say nothing," interposed our visitor, "of the first—the very first—score of Tartini's *Trillo.*"

"He has asked me to dine with him to-morrow or next day—it must for the moment be doubtful which—when he will tell us a curious history concerning it."

Here again the visitor interposed to explain with much courtesy that he would be very glad if I would come too. As it happened, I was engaged for both the days mentioned, but for the life of me I could not say so, and felt impelled, with my knees loosened like those of all the Latins with dismay, to murmur an expression of thanks.

" If you will kindly give me your address," said the stranger, " I will write about the day and hour as soon as I get back to my hotel ; " and with these words he produced a tiny gold-clasped *carnet*, the meaning of which I knew only too well.

Once again my unwilling fingers were on the point of signing, when the curtain rose on the wayside cross beside which Alice sits, and the traveller vanished with a suddenness and instantaneousness which seemed not to surprise my friend. When I referred afterwards to the fact that the door had not opened, that our visitor had not climbed down the boxes, and that yet he had certainly left us in a second, my friend said—

" Ah, queer fellow—great traveller—up to all kinds of dodges." And as to the truth of the last statement I had no manner of doubt.

The dinner I took pains to avoid by throwing over all my engagements and going down to see a friend in the country the next day. The journey was a long one, and I made friends at its beginning with the guard, who got me a carriage to myself. During one of the stoppages, at about 7.45 in the evening, and just as the train was about to start, I found that I had dropped my cigar-case and match-box. I was about to see if there were yet time to communicate with my friend the guard, and through him get from the refreshment-room whatever they might have in the way of tobacco, when a stranger stepped nimbly into the carriage, a bell was rung, the engine-driver whistled, and the train started. The first act of the stranger, at whom, annoyed at my seclusion being broken, I did not look, was to say—

" You have lost your cigar-case and match-box; let me supply the deficiency."

I was by this time so accustomed to the unexpected, that the remark seemed to me a merely ordinary piece of civility, and so much off my guard was I that I watched with lazy interest the stranger's hand, as it produced an enormous chest of cigars and hundreds of match-boxes from a very exiguous hand-bag.

"These," said the stranger, as I took a cigar, "are curious matches. They are called the pen-match, or, if you prefer it, the match-pen, which comes as a boon and a blessing to men. They have been lately patented, and their merit is that they will write on the solid darkness. Conceive the saving of time! Let me show you." With this he struck a match, which burnt with a dull red glow, and blew out (through its glass shade) the carriage lamp. "Now," he continued, " see if you cannot write your name on this admirable sheet of darkness."

By this time I was awake to the situation, and in the folly and the horror of the moment I flew straight at the stranger's throat. No sooner had I done so than the whole roof of the carriage fell with a mighty crash around me, leaving me, but for a few bruises, unhurt, but pilloried, so to speak, among the fragments, which formed a kind of collar round my neck, that held me motionless. Directly afterwards the train stopped, some one in the adjoining carriage, horrified at the crash, having pulled the cord, and my friend the guard came to my assistance. When, with great difficulty, he had extricated me, he said, not unnaturally, " Why the devil must have been in this carriage." To which I still less unnaturally replied, " That is exactly what he was."

Struck by the calmness with which I said this the guard looked at me, and observing that I was no doubt a bit shaken, begged me to stop at the next station, only five miles off, and put up at an excellent hotel kept by a connection of his own. This I foolishly consented to do, wishing to rest after my latest adventure ; and I accordingly had my traps carried to " The Crown." The house looked comfortable ; the landlady was full of sympathy, and the bill of fare was full of excellent things. I looked forward to the refreshment of a good night's rest, when the good-natured looking hostess came bustling up to me and asked me to write my name in the visitor's book. I am bound to say that on this occasion my suspicions may have been entirely unfounded, but not the less I fled precipitately, leaving the people of the house to think that my head was affected by my late accident. When I got back to town in the morning, I sought out my operatic friend, and said to him :

"I suppose you dined with Mand—with your friend the captain, last night ?"

"Yes," he replied ; "we missed you much —and by the way, he said, oddly enough, as we sat down to dinner, that he hoped you were having a pleasant journey. Have you been away ?"

To which I answered feebly enough, " I don't know."

After this, I was left for some time in peace. Possibly " my illustrious friend " had other fish to fry. Anyhow, I had practically banished the whole matter from my mind, having set it down to nerves, liver, over-work, anything that would account for its unreality, when one day as I was working in my study, correcting some proof-sheets which Morton had submitted to my judgment, concerning superstitions, which, for a wonder, were still a favourite subject with him, my servant announced that a gentleman wished to see me on particular business. I was not sorry to interrupt my work for a moment. The gentleman, whose name on his card I recognised as that of an active member of a religious sect, was shown up. His face was almost entirely hidden by a luxurious growth of hair ; but what little of it was visible was pitted with small-pox marks. He had come to me to speak about a certain religious movement, on which I had been writing. He paid me many compliments, and put before me certain arguments on what I had always thought the wrong side, the cogency and brilliancy of which struck me with amazement. Presently, he was so good as to ask for my autograph—

which he said he would value much in the distant shores to which he was returning. I was flattered, and was about to write it, when I saw his attention caught by a curious cross-handled dagger, which was revealed by my moving some papers which had concealed it. I gave him some account of its history, to which he listened in a *distrait* manner, and then, harking back to theology, talked so rapidly and brilliantly on subjects connected with the proof-sheets before me, that I forgot for a time his request for the autograph. This, however, I finally wrote, as he had asked, in the form of a letter on the subject he had at heart, and still talking or listening, put it in an envelope, and bent over it to seal it with a signet attached to the cross-handled dagger, saying at the same time—

"You think, then, that there is no such thing as a personal devil ?"

I got no answer, and when I looked up,

surprised, my visitor had vanished. Looking out of my window, I saw him sitting on a hill a quarter of a mile off, and heard him say in a voice which I now remembered only too well—

" Pardon me, I never said anything of the sort."

In spite of myself, I replied, without raising my voice, but with an immense feeling of relief, " Good-bye ; " to which he answered, as he disappeared over the brow of the hill—

" O dear no ! *Au plaisir de vous revoir !*"

It was a considerable time after the events just recorded that I got a letter from an old and favourite aunt of mine in the country speaking of a friend of hers, a certain Lady Volant, of whom I had never before heard, and asking for my help on this friend's behalf. Lady Volant, it seemed, was in legal difficulties of a delicate kind with regard to the behaviour of some of her family, and, of course, this behaviour concerned the disposition of property.

Before taking any definite step she was most anxious to consult some one who could be entirely trusted, who would give an unbiassed opinion, and who would, after hearing all the circumstances, point out what solicitor, if any, would be best fitted to take the matter up. Though I had practically left the bar, my aunt thought I could probably advise Lady Volant as to a solicitor, and, as it happened, I could. She also not only thought but felt sure that I was just the person to deal with so delicate a matter—which was flattering. "Would I," she asked, in conclusion, " do her a personal favour by calling next day on Lady Volant [at an address in the wilds of St. John's Wood] at eleven in the morning?"

The undertaking was peculiarly inconvenient, but I owed my aunt a debt of much kindness, and with a light-heartedness which seldom deserts me made up my mind to the sacrifice of a day. Had I known how the day would be spent I might have been less light-hearted.

I started next morning in one of the gondolas of London, and was driven to the

s

house indicated in St. John's Wood. It was a house with a strip of ground and a few blades of grass in front of it, and with an outer door, shut, to guard this ground. At the bell of this door I had just rung when my cabman, bending down confidentially said, in a cabman's whisper—

"I think, sir, you'll find them waiting for you inside."

I was, I confess, surprised; but thought it meet to say "thank you" in a common-place way, and walk through the garden door which suddenly stood open instead of being shut. The cabman had spoken truly. The house-door was also wide open and "they" in the shape of a most respectable footman stood waiting for me inside.

"Is Lady Volant at home?" I asked, expecting an immediate "Yes, sir." What I got was a critical examination from head to foot, and the words, "I will see, sir," delivered, as it seemed to me, with a curiously sarcastic intonation.

The footman then left me standing at one end of a long hall, lighted with painted windows, and himself disappeared at the other end of it. No sooner was his back turned than the whistles of speaking tubes began to sound in shrill succession all around me, while strange tootings of horns and scrapings of strings, as of a fiend-children's concert, were heard over head. This lasted without intermission for five minutes, at the end of which the footman reappeared at the other end of the hall running rapidly. He ran down the hall, he ran past me, he ran to the front door which he flung open with eagerness. He gazed painfully round the strip of ground, and then exchanging his run for an amble, he returned to me and said—

"I beg your pardon, sir, she is not at home."

What with the noise of horns and fiddles, the constant whistling, and the strangeness of the whole thing I felt so bewildered that I found nothing better to say than, "Oh, thank you," with which words I took up my hat. As I did so innumerable gongs of incredible sonorousness seemed to be struck with one accord in every corner of the house, and amidst their over-powering din I made my way back to my friendly cabman, who, as soon as I was in the cab, drove off.

It did not occur to me that he had started without knowing, or at any rate without asking, where we were going. As we went on I got more and more annoyed and bored at what had happened, and when after we had covered about half a mile he asked through the trap door—

" Where shall I drive you, sir ? "

I answered petulantly, " Oh, drive me where you like—drive me to the ——."

At that moment a shrill voice cried, "Stop ! pray stop !" The cabman pulled up, and I, looking out, saw close beside us a huge hansom cab, painted black with scarlet wheels, containing a very small page, who flourished an envelope frantically towards me. I leant out, took it from him, and found that it contained a telegram from my aunt addressed to me at the house I had just left, and couched in these words—

" Inexplicable mistake. Very sorry to trouble you. Lady Volant at 10, Boulogne Villas, Peacock Road Station. Pray follow her. Trains every twenty minutes from Euston."

" Very well," I said, in a leaden, mechanical way to the page boy, " I will go."

"Thank you, sir," he replied, with infinite respect, mingled as I thought on after reflection with an impish malevolence.

So far the events which had befallen me were certainly odd enough; but then my aunt, charming as she was, was eccentric, and it was natural that her friends should be eccentric. Not for a moment did I dream of associating this day's events with any of my previous experiences. I simply accepted what seemed to me the inevitable, and took a train as the telegram directed to Peacock Road Station, as to which all I knew was that it belonged to a new suburb.

When I got there I found a large station, a station full of interweaving lines and multitudinous platforms, a station which was a vast expanse of pavement and railroad, and in which not a single human being was to be discerned. I was consumed with an honest desire to deliver up my ticket, but I could see no one to whom by any possibility it could be delivered up, until in a corner I came upon a lampman sitting dreamily on a bench and smoking a long German pipe. This was odd, but it was not odder than the rest; and the black hansom, and the page, and the whole thing seemed to hang well enough together, so that I merely said to him —

"I want to give up this ticket."

"Yes, sir," he replied, without moving, "you may just as well give it to me as anybody else;" and against this proposition I had nothing to offer.

When he had taken the ticket I felt emboldened to ask him where Boulogne Villas were, and he replied that they were a matter of a mile and a half off. This, as the day was fine, and as he gave me very clear directions as to the route, was not much of a misfortune, and I started for Boulogne Villas, little thinking of the wisdom, which I had before and have since so much respected, of Mr. Toobad's philosophy. My way lay through that cheerless waste belonging to new suburbs, which is all the more cheerless because of its unfinished jauntiness. It had the germ of a mock gaiety and a mock sociable aspect about it. The builder's boards rising on thin black poles from brick-strewn ground and vaunting it as the site of an eligible residence or of a "winter garden with unparalleled attractions," reminded one, but with a difference, of Balzac's imaginary decorations of his rooms. It had more of the essence of suburbanism than it could possibly have when the houses were actually built, and it was depressing enough to a mind trained by the philosophy of the day to deal with essences. This, however,

I could endure. What I found it less easy to endure was the sight of a placard upon which I presently came, and of which the full horror can be appreciated only by those whose fortune or misfortune it has been to study the works of Bullen and Leake, and other legal hand-books.

The placard was hung over the entrance to a half finished arcade, built on the model of the Albany, and bore these mystic and terrifying words, "The Involuntary Bailee has strict orders to supply all householders with every key of every door, and every door of every key." The mixture of apparently sound common sense and of obviously appalling folly in this announcement fairly staggered me, and when I had read it twice I began to resume my walk hastily, thinking that to eat no breakfast and to smoke a great many cigarettes was no doubt a bad thing, but filled not the less with the firm belief that I had read the inscription aright, and that the folly was not in me, but in some mad fellow who had put it up in a waggishness. Indeed when I had gone about a hundred yards further I felt irresistibly impelled to go back again and see the matter of this placard so far as might be to its end.

Advancing to what looked like a porter's lodge at the entrance of the arcade, I found behind a hastily run up glass door, a little squat, commonplace man, with an odd air of newness—just such a man as fitted such a place.

" Are you," I asked him, without a moment's hesitation, " the Involuntary Bailee ? "

He replied in the most matter-of-fact way that he was, and his tone was of so ordinary a kind that I felt no emotion but curiosity.

This, however, I felt so strongly that—
Heaven forgive me for lying!—I proceeded
to say that I wished to know all about the
arcade, as I was thinking of taking rooms
there. He then went into questions of rent
and so forth, and ended by asking if I would
leave my name and address with him in order
that he might send me further and better
particulars, producing at the same time a
book in which I might inscribe myself.
Constitutional stupidity was at the moment
so strong with me that I merely reflected
that it might be a bore to be let in for a
correspondence, and told him that I would
think the matter over, and would write to
him.

On receiving this answer he glanced at me
literally like a fiend, and I must ask to be
believed when I state that even this had no
effect upon my mind. There is a well-

known proverb about a long spoon; but, perhaps, it is possible for one's host to provide for his own purposes a spoon somewhat too long, a spoon which passes harmlessly over the head of the person that it is meant to catch up.   Anyhow, it is sure that mere bewilderment—allied, as I have said, with a certain ingrained dulness—availed for a long time on this remarkable morning to make me accept with indifference, or, at least, with a mild wonder, whatever befell me, and, it may be, thus to avoid various pitfalls.

About a quarter of a mile from the arcade I came upon a bridge with a toll-bar. The keeper of this toll-bar was a man of gigantic stature, whose legs and feet came out of his hut, while his body and arms remained inside.   On one foot he wore a stocking of thin stuff, divided into separate toe-caps.

These he stretched out to receive my toll, and acting on I know not what impulse I put into his foot the sum of fivepence-halfpenny. He then said—and I have since thought that it was a stupid thing for him to say—

"If you had not had the right sum with you, you would have had to write your name in my book."

I looked at him, however, in vacant amazement, and went on my way.

On the other side of the bridge was a neat-looking roadside inn, and as by this time I was somewhat tired, dusty, and thirsty I turned into the bar to ask for a glass of beer. The landlord, as I supposed, a rubicund, jovial kind of person, came shuffling up to me, and asked me if I would not go into the parlour, where I could sit down and be more at ease. I readily assented, and he then promised to bring me in a glass of a very particular kind of ale, which it was not everybody who could appreciate. It was kept at the very back of the cellar, and it would, he feared, take him a minute or two to get it up; but, perhaps, I would not mind that.

I did not mind in the least; and while the host was gone I amused myself in an absent, mechanical way by scribbling my name with a pen on a piece of blank paper, as I thought, which lay beside me on the table. Just as I signed my name for the third time I heard a slight noise behind me, and turning my head perceived that my host had re-entered, carrying a jug and a glass, by a door at my back.

He looked even more pleased and jovial than before, and prepared to set down the glass. I stretched out my hand to take it from him, with a word of thanks; and as I did so a lighted cigarette dropped from my fingers, fell upon the paper which I had covered with my signature, and set it in a blaze. I tried to extinguish it, but was too late; it was completely burned up. The host stood as if glued to his place, he trembled from head to foot, his eyes rolled, and he cried in a kind of roaring whisper—

"Has! has! my dinkorlitz!"

The words immediately started in me a train of recollection. He must have seen this in my face, for he immediately recovered himself, overwhelmed me with assurances that the paper was valueless—I had afterwards reason to believe that whatever its value to him its destruction was of very great moment to me—gave some nonsensical but plausible explanation of the odd language he had used, and succeeded in so flustering me that, so to speak, he stamped out the spark of memory before the train it was laid to was well alight. It was not till afterwards that I remembered where the words came from, and how I happened to be acquainted with them.

"You said," I proceeded to observe, "that this was particularly good beer."

"And so it is, sir," he replied, filling the glass from the jug; "none know it better than I do."

With this he drank off at a gulp the liquor, which went hissing down his throat, and disappeared with incredible swiftness through an open door. Nor on following him could I find any trace either of him or of any other living creature in the house.

Pursuing my bewildered way in the direction pointed out to me by the friendly lamp-man at the station, I presently arrived at Boulogne Villas, and rang at the door where

I had been told to look for Lady Volant. The bell was immediately answered in a somewhat unexpected way by a servant, who ascended the steps from behind my back, unbolted the door from the front, entered the house, and then assumed the conventional attitude of a footman who opens a door.

"Is Lady Volant at home?" I inquired.

"I do not know, sir," replied the fellow, with a strong French accent; "but if you will come in I will inquire. Sir Volant, I know, is here."

I let him show me into a drawing-room, and while he was away fell to wondering whether Frenchmen would ever learn to interpret English titles correctly, and to wondering what the baptismal name before Volant could be—that there was no Lord Volant I knew.

"Sir Volant," I repeated to myself, "Sir

T

Volant—how ridiculous it seems ; but, surely, I have seen the name somewhere before. Where can it have been ? ''

At this moment a stately, sad-looking personage, who seemed to walk somewhat stiffly, entered the room, and, greeting me courteously, while he thanked me greatly for coming, explained that Lady Volant was suffering from a severe headache, and had asked him to be her interpreter. The man interested me strangely, the more because I could not rid myself of a notion that I had seen him somewhere before; but he had given me no direct clue as to his personality although I felt sure he was the French servant's " Sir Volant."

" I have the pleasure," I said, " of speaking to "—

" Exactly," he replied, and motioning me to a chair, sat down hastily, and pulled out a bundle of papers. From these, having explained that the proceeding was necessary for the understanding of Lady Volant's case, he began to read in a droning, grating voice, which, in spite of its jarring quality, had a decidedly soporific tendency, while his words and phrases seemed to me ever to contain some strange and fateful meaning which I could not fully discern. At last the name "Volant" struck heavily on my ear, through a jumble of sounding clauses, and I exclaimed hastily, without a second's reflection—

"Your Christian name, you say, is"—

The reader bent upon me one withering look of hatred and scorn, and resumed his reading as if nothing had happened. For me I fell back in a sort of numb silence. More and more tortuous grew the reader's phraseology, and, as Herr von Wolzogen says of the *motif* for Fafner *(als Wurm)* in the Nibelung's Ring trilogy, more and more "heavy and snake-like its windings." It seemed to me that I was ringed and en-wrapped with bewildering convolutions of sonorous nonsense, but that it was, mayhap, my own stupidity that made it seem nonsense. All the time the reader kept his black, piercing eyes fixed steadily on me. At length he stopped, and, passing over a sheet of paper to me, said—

"In short, if you will sign your name there the whole thing will be settled."

And so, no doubt, it might have been. Stupidly I took the pen, stupidly I was about to sign, when I looked up and saw in the reader's eyes a look of malignant triumph, that I now remembered but too well. Suddenly the whole thing flashed upon me. What was the "Has! has! my dinkorlitz!"

of the innkeeper but a fragment of Sweden-
borg's fiend-language—how was it that the
voice of the reader and the name of Sir
Volant seemed familiar to me ?   I leaped to
my feet, and cried wildly—

"Sir Volant—Sir Volant! ah!   I remember now the words in the Walpurgis
night scene of *Faust*—ah ! I know you now !"

On the instant the reader's face changed.
The eyes kept their piercing blackness and
youth, while the skin shrivelled into wrinkles
and grew to a dull parchment hue, and with
this the countenance wore an aspect of
immeasurable and terrifying anger.   He
advanced towards me with a long, livid
hand outstretched.   I fled towards the door.
The hand pursued me.   I doubled back to
to the window, and there was the hand,
interposed between the glass and me, while
the crackling sound of the reader's low toned

laughter came from the furthermost corner of the vast room. Suddenly—as such things will come to one at strange times—I murmured a few words of a Zulu exorcism which I had picked up from a travelled friend.

The laughter ceased, the hand vanished. I dashed open the French window with my foot, and rushed on to the lawn unhurt through the shivering glass. Once there, I ran as hard as I could to the station, and was carried back to town without any further manifestation of the diabolical persecution from which I had suffered. As soon as I got to my rooms I looked for my aunt's letter. It had disappeared, which surprised me but little.

Two days later I met her, and took an occasion of asking her if she knew Lady Volant. My aunt—I have said she is eccentric—replied, with some asperity—

"Lady Volant? No. I don't believe there's any such person. And if there was, I wouldn't touch her with a pair of tongs."

I reflected that, supposing the acquaintance possible, the tongs would probably be in the hands of the other party to it ; but this reflection I thought it prudent to keep to myself.

THE END.

Printed by Remington & Co., 134, New Bond Street, W.

9 783337 332495